DARUMA DAYS

OTHER WORKS BY TERRY WATADA

Bukkyō Tōzen: A History of Jōdo Shinshū Buddhism in Canada,
1905–1995
HpF Press and the Toronto Buddhist Church, 1996

Face Kao: Portraits of Japanese Canadians Interned During WWII,
Andrew Danson Editor, HpF Press, 1996

A Thousand Homes (poetry),
The Mercury Press, 1995

"The Tale of a Mask" *Canadian Mosaic* (play anthology),
Aviva Ravel ed., Simon & Pierre, 1995

Asian Voices: Stories from Canada, Korea, China, Vietnam and Japan,
Anthology Editor, HpF Press and the
North York Board of Education, 1993

DARUMA DAYS

A Collection of Fictionalised Biography

Terry Watada

RONSDALE
1997

RONSDALE PRESS
3350 West 21st Avenue
Vancouver, BC, Canada
V6S 1G7

Set in Bembo, 12/14
Typeset by The Typeworks, Vancouver, BC
Printing: Hignell Printing, Winnipeg, Manitoba
Cover Art: Alvin Jang
Cover Design: Cecilia Jang
Author Photo: Phil Doi

The publisher wishes to thank the Canada Council, the Department of Heritage and the British Columbia Cultural Services Branch for their financial assistance.

CANADIAN CATALOGUING-IN-PUBLICATION DATA

Watada, Terry
Daruma days

ISBN 0-921870-43-4

1. Japanese Canadians—Evacuation and relocation, 1942–1945—Fiction.*   I. Title.
PS8595.A79D37   1997   C813'.54   C97-910010-0
PR9199.3.W3688D37   1997

For
the issei and nisei ghosts

Acknowledgements

I thank the following for their confidence in me, for their love and friendship, and for their stories: Tane Akamatsu, Michael Burrell, Dr. Wes Fujiwara, Roy and Kay Honda, Dorothy Kagawa, Joy Kogawa, Frank Moritsugu, Robin Muller, Yuki Nakamura, Jesse Nishihata, Tom Oyagi, Kay Shin, Rosemary Stackhouse, Gloria Sumiya, Saburo Takahashi, Mayu Takasaki, Toyo Takata, Yusuke and Deirdre Tanaka, Rev. Kenryu Tsuji, Saeko Usukawa, Tamio Wakayama, Dr. Brian Watada, GT Wong, Leslee Inaba Wong, Asia Wong, Jim Wong Chu, Harry Yonekura and Ed Yoshida.

I wish to acknowledge the Toronto Arts Council Grants to Writers Program for its generous financial support. I also want to thank Ronald and Veronica Hatch for their commitment to the book and the editorial push in pointing out all the possibilities, and to George Payerle for the conversation, the editing and the insights into the Canadian writing community.

Some of the stories appeared in *Grain, Antigonish Review, White Wall Review* and *MoonRabbit Review.*

The poems "The Bodhidharma ...", "the chatter ...", and *Another Home: 1959 Japan* were written by T. Watada, © 1997.

Kojō-no Tsuki: lyrics by Bansai Doi, music by Rentaro Taki, 1900.

Contents

A Note on Language

Because most of the characters in *Daruma Days* speak both Japanese and English, and often switch back and forth between the two, the representation of spoken language has presented a challenge. Since it would have been tedious always to mention which language is being spoken, the following convention has been employed. When characters are speaking English but incorporating Japanese expressions, these words are placed in italics; when it is to be assumed that characters are speaking Japanese, Japanese words are *not* placed in italics (except for emphasis). In narrative passages, of course, Japanese and other non-English words are italicized, as is customary.

The Daruma

The Bodhidharma
sat in silent meditation.
Enlightenment was his!

But he fell asleep
— once only.

Upon awakening,
he flew into a fit of rage
and cut off his eyelids.

He sat for nine years
contemplating
his life of suffering.
Slowly, one by one,
limbs fell
until he became the daruma,
the one who never sleeps,
the one
*   who never falls.*

Perseverance —
the Buddha's eyelids grew as the first tea plant.

Atsuko Hatanaka was extremely calm for what she had in mind. Although the sun had not yet set, the basement apartment had grown dark; the air thick. Still, she could see the dust mingling with the light which came in from the one small ground-level window.

The half-finished basement contained a laundry room, furnace area and her bedroom furnished with an easy chair, end tables and the prerequisite Sony TV. She ate her meals with her dentist son's family upstairs in the light and free air of the kitchen.

Around her arm, the eighty-year-old woman slung a lariat of skipping-rope that her grandchild had left carelessly strewn across the basement steps. It was green with yellow handles. She stretched a portion of it. "It's strong enough," she whispered.

She looked around her room for something else, something specific. She had one task left before she proceeded with her intentions. The photographs, Japanese ornaments, *kokeshi* dolls, framed scriptures, and loose change. Not here, not there.

Her darting eyes finally landed upon a small figurine. The bright red *daruma*, round with a flat base to keep it upright, sat defiant, its white face fierce with expressive black ink strokes. One eye was blank, the other filled in crudely with a child's crayon.

She grabbed hold of it and uttered a curse, inadvertently spitting at the angry features of the *papier-mâché* talisman. Her own face suffused with blood as she raised it above her head. With a violent snap of her arm, she flung it across the room.

The *daruma* lay damaged, a crack splitting its face. She stood paralysed in the subsiding of emotion and the surging of memory. Her breathing became heavy, her eyes glowed.

★

As a young woman, Atsuko had never considered herself a beauty. She was a small woman with a homely face and a formless

3

body prone to illness. She had never thought she could attract a
man. Her mother had not thought so either and had told her as
much before packing her off to care for an ailing aunt in Canada. It
was there under unusual circumstances that Atsuko came to meet
her future husband: Bunjiro Hatanaka, the local *nombei*, the town
drunk. Atsuko found him in a heap on her lawn six months after
her aunt had died. He had collapsed in the freezing January rain in
a drunken stupor in front of her house. She helped him to his feet
and took him in, perhaps out of pity. More likely, she missed the
routine of caring for someone on a daily basis. Her aunt had lasted
almost two years after Atsuko had arrived.

As he lay on the davenport in the front living room, Atsuko
caught a glimpse of a handsome face below the dissipated surface.
The eyelids had withered to a permanently sad droop. The nose,
long and prominent, was broken in more than one place. The jaw
remained sharp, crusted with rashes that interrupted the line.

Her first task was to bathe him. She felt no embarrassment as she
stripped him of his rags which steamed in the hallway air. The hot
water rushed around his emaciated body as she eased him into the
tub. The shock woke him to full consciousness for a moment but
soon his body relaxed and he fell asleep.

In the days that followed, she fed him *okayu*, a watery rice soup
reminiscent of white glue. It did the trick; he gathered strength in
her care. He soon became strong enough to talk. During the dull
rainy afternoons, he spoke at length on various subjects – especially
his personal history.

"I shouldn't have come to Canada," he confessed in an understated Japanese. "Nothing but misery here."

Atsuko sensed a revelation and looked away, wishing not to em-
barrass him.

"I had no choice, I suppose. My life in Japan ... well, I started
badly there," he admitted tentatively. "You know the expression
'tatakeiba hokoriga detekuru'? Well, slap my back and a whole
mountain of dust would come out." He gave a laugh before stifling
himself, his skin a flush of pink.

Atsuko was intrigued. Not so much by the possibility of past scandal but by his manner, his honesty. She did not press for more – that would be indiscreet.

In the weeks that followed, she listened quietly while attending to his needs. He was only too happy to talk. No one, it seemed, had ever listened to him before.

Before immigrating, Bunjiro Hatanaka lived in relative luxury with his family in Hiroshima Prefecture, Japan. As a second son, he was entitled to very little as inheritance except boat fare to Canada and a chance to prove himself in a management position with a Japanese logging concern in Vancouver.

While working for the Toyama Lumber Company, Bunjiro met and wedded, through the negotiating skills of a local *baishakunin*, the boss's daughter – a diminutive eighteen-year-old with a mousy face and a strict sense of propriety.

Getting married in the Japanese community was a simple matter. Once the two families agreed to the union, the groom had the relatives in Japan register his bride's name in the family temple and that was that. There wasn't any ceremony, civil or religious – in fact, the Canadian legal system wasn't even aware a wedding had taken place.

Bunjiro, himself a young man at twenty, saw this union as a good one when he considered his past, something he never disclosed in the marriage negotiations. And so, after he had sent word to his family in Japan to pay a visit to the temple, he and his bride attended a grand reception, put on by his father-in-law, the Toyama Company's owner and *taisho*, to mark the occasion.

The couple was happy for a while, but Bunjiro soon found the responsibilities and expectations of married life overwhelming. He took to drinking, gambling and womanising.

Etsuji Morii, Black Dragon leader of Vancouver's Little Tokyo, offered much encouragement. "Hatanaka-san," hissed Morii, "why don't you come down to the Raku Raku? Good drink there."

Bunjiro looked at the little man adorned with coke-bottle glasses and pencil-thin moustache. "No. I can't. My wife's expecting me at home."

"Eh? The wife got you on a chain? Are you a little boy?" Morii squeezed his eyes into smiles. "Listen, the women at the Raku Raku might just be more to your liking – these women will treat you like a man!" Bunjiro hesitated for but a moment.

After a time, the drunken fits, the mounting debts and the nagging gossip prompted his wife to consider divorce. The last straw was the incident at her parents' household.

Bunjiro had been drinking for most of the evening. On the advice of a devil, he decided to pay a visit to his *taisho* father-in-law.

With great bravado, he stormed the steps of the detached two-storey house on Powell Street in Little Tokyo, bellowing his boss's name.

The noise was so great, the entire household came out to the veranda.

"What the hell are you doing, Hatanaka?" shouted the angry Toyama *taisho*. "Go home to your wife, you drunken idiot."

Bunjiro raised his arm in protest and almost said something he would surely have regretted later. Fortunately, all he projected was vomit. The charm of Mrs. Toyama's abundant tulips withered in the assault.

Bunjiro's wife wanted a divorce. Toyama *taisho*, despite the shame attached, agreed to look into it.

Getting married was simple – but divorce? The community considered it dishonourable. If compelling reasons emerged, then everyone could accept the estrangement, but Bunjiro's dissipated ways were not reason enough. Many husbands indulged in such activities.

Still, Bunjiro eventually received a *mi kudari han* from his wife, a three-line note declaring annulment. It was unusual for a woman to send such a note, and people raised their eyes in surprise. They soon guessed why all parties had agreed: the family name was at stake. Bunjiro, in his case, had no choice but to agree, especially when Toyama *taisho* revealed to him privately what he had learned from a *baishakunin* in Japan. An invisible hand hit his back and the dust of secrets flew. *Hokoriga detekita.*

Throughout the weeks Atsuko tended to Bunjiro's needs and listened attentively, keeping her own counsel. Finally, she sensed a lull in his monologue and made the decision to speak.

"Hatanaka-san? What will you do once you're strong enough?"

Bunjiro raised his head slowly. He had not considered that possibility. "I don't know. I suppose I shouldn't let my good fortune go to waste. I'll get a job in a sawmill."

"You'd be good at it!" Atsuko answered smiling.

"I'd make something of myself, that's for sure. No more drinking!"

"I know what you should do to ensure that promise."

"What's that?"

"You should marry. You should marry *me*!"

The look of astonishment on Bunjiro's face froze like a photograph in Atsuko's mind. She could see he had not considered matrimony.

Bunjiro couldn't believe what he was hearing. However, it was true, this small, attentive woman paid him every kindness. "Marry?"

"You need a strong wife," Atsuko boldly interjected, "to keep you from drinking, to keep you healthy. I am that wife."

Bunjiro thought about his present state. "Why would you want to marry me? Open yourself to all that gossip?"

"Oh, it'll be bad at first, but eventually ..." Atsuko's voice faded as she turned to a nearby mirror. The round face with sunken eyes, stringy hair and weak chin stared at her in disbelief. *What are you saying?* The conviction in her voice wavered.

"So be it," proclaimed Bunjiro abruptly. "Let's get married. I need a wife, you need a husband. So be it."

Atsuko bowed without emotion. Bunjiro did the same. A deal had been struck. A fate sealed.

As predicted, the gossip was pernicious during the days following the sad wedding party at Atsuko's house. *It's shameful the way
they carry on. She asked him, you know. So desperate. Him, divorced in
disgrace. You know what they say about him at the church? Hatanaka-san
wa tatakeiba hokoriga detekuru. I think he had an affair with a married
woman before he came here! No. That's what I heard.*

Despite the speculation about Bunjiro's past in Japan and the
controversy surrounding their union, marriage agreed with them.
Bunjiro gave up drinking almost immediately. He worked hard as a
miner, then as a logger and finally as a fisherman. It was the last oc-
cupation that yielded for him, Atsuko and their new-born son a
cottage home up an inlet of Vancouver Island.

There, life prospered. He eventually bought his own fishing boat
and every day put out to sea to reap the ocean's harvest. Atsuko
busied herself with household chores, looked after her son Toshio
and gave birth to their second son, Yoji.

Happiness seemed a permanent state, until the summer of 1940.

★

The whir of memory reverberated throughout her body. She
collapsed face-down on the bed. When she felt the white sheet
grow wet beneath her, she sat up and touched the wrinkled skin
beneath her eyes. The area was swollen with emotion.

She clutched the skipping rope close to her. "Life is so hard," she
screamed almost incoherently. She threw herself to the bed again.
"Why is life so hard?" Her voice was soon reduced to hiccuped
crying until it faded into the silence of sleep.

★

It was a hot August morning. Bunjiro had sailed before day-
break to reach his fishing grounds. Atsuko spent the morning in
the shed cleaning out the *kasu* that caked the walls of the *koji*.
The previous night she had begun the process of making another
batch of bootleg *sake*. A batch yielded ten bottles of burning

white alcohol, the kind loggers and miners liked to drink to melt the tension of hard work. As always, she planned to sell the merchandise down on Powell Street in Vancouver when next they took a trip to town.

The extra money helped them afford some decorative things for the cottage; with the profit from a previous batch, she had bought a *daruma*, a colourful egg-round representation of a Buddha that was said to bring good luck to the home.

During a break from her cleaning, Atsuko retrieved the ornament from the bedroom and sat at the kitchen table with it in the palm of her hand. While sipping her cup of tea, she recalled contemplating the wisdom of the purchase the day she bought it. The red figure came with a fierce face and no eyes, only blank white spaces. Superstition dictated that its owner fill in one eye when she had a wish. When it came true, she was to fill in the other eye. She thought the trinket an unnecessary purchase. The money could have been more usefully put towards supplies. But the *daruma* reminded her of her childhood in Japan.

At bedtime, her mother had often told her the story of the warrior monk who one day decided the way to Enlightenment was through continuous meditation. For days and then months, he demonstrated his perseverance by sitting absolutely still. He felt his suffering would gain him Enlightenment. Unfortunately, his desire for it caused him to suffer in a different way.

One night, he unexpectedly fell asleep, interrupting his concentration – ruining his quest. When he awoke, he flew into a fury and tore off his eyelids so that he would never again sleep and break the spell of his meditation. The eyelids grew into the first tea plant. Thus, with the taste of tea, the drinker will know that the Buddha is near.

The monk then began again. The months turned into years but never did he move. Eventually, his limbs fell off one by one until he was the perfection of *gaman* – one that never sleeps, one that never falls. In the end, he learned one thing in particular: all beings suffer and that suffering comes from within. To end suffering all desire must be eliminated.

The *daruma* thus became a symbol for perseverance and later, mistakenly, for good luck which in itself can cause suffering.

Atsuko finished her tea. As she had no wish at the moment, she left the warrior Buddha white-blind on top of the bedroom bureau and returned to her chores in the outside shed.

The remnants she scraped from the fermenting tub would make an excellent marinade. The *sake* aroma to a meal had to satisfy her husband, for no bottles were ever left behind that might become too much of a temptation.

While she toiled, her sons walked along the sea-wall at the bottom of the front yard. After playing pirates on the bed of the family pickup and exploring the pier for dry-docked creatures, there was little else to do. Toshio, the *onīsan* with strong legs and sprouting height, was charged with looking after his little brother while his parents worked. He resented the responsibility and told his brother to "get lost" from time to time. Yoji paid no attention to the admonishments and playfully tripped along behind his truculent big brother.

From the wall, Toshio looked across the sea which undulated gently with small waves. The water was at low tide, clear as a child's eyes. It came upon him to make a wish. His bowl-cut hair tousled in the slight wind as he squeezed his thinly slitted eyes shut. He placed his hands across the stomach of his checkered shirt and wished for a catalogue toy. A moment later, he popped his eyes open as a ripple of laughter sounded. "What was that?" he questioned out loud. Another chuckle. He looked in several directions and saw nothing, but his stomach began to tingle. The sensation quickly spread until it needled every part of his body. A sudden premonition occurred to him. He tilted his head toward the sun to blind himself of it. He bellowed in a loud trembling voice at the dread that was accumulating in his being.

A splash came from behind. Toshio snapped his head around. The landscape burned with sunspots. When his vision cleared, he found his brother missing. He looked straight down and saw Yoji lying in the water, moving only when the waves willed it.

Toshio tore open the shed's crude door calling to his mother in crippled Japanese and English. "*Kāsan, kochi* come *ne*! Yoji ... Yoji. Something happened!"

Her dress ruffled as Atsuko swept herself up and rushed to the sea-wall. Nothing appeared wrong at first. Then on the other side of the wall, she found Yoji's body face down in eight inches of water. Atsuko desperately took him up in her arms and turned him over. A large gash crossed Yoji's forehead. A nearby rock was smeared with blood. A mask was forming over his face. She sank her face into the soft wet folds of his clothes. Her body shook in sorrow and horror.

Toshio stood frozen in place, his stomach knotted, his limbs weak and numb. He was alone, replaying the events in his mind.

> *Amida Butsu kokowo sarukoto tōkarasu.*
> Amida Buddha exists not far from you.

The compassionate minister in black robe and tie coughed gently to begin the chanting that involved the living and committed the dead. The funeral had been small with only the immediate family attending. The seventh-day observance, being held in the little cottage on Vancouver Island, included several guests that had to be repaid for some past kindness. A cousin arranged for the food, snacks of *manju* and cake paid for by the sale of ten bottles of the bootleg *dobuzake*. Atsuko sat with a long pale face and gripped her *ojuzu* with white knuckles until the blood drained from her hands.

Toshio was nowhere to be found.

"Don't blame the child," Atsuko had said to her distraught husband the day after the drowning.

"It was his responsibility as oldest brother," Bunjiro scolded.

"It wasn't his fault."

"That's the problem with you. You're too soft! He is onīsan! It is his fault," he reiterated as he pulled his belt through the pant loops.

"Perhaps," Atsuko sighed.

The boy clawed at the white sand of his favourite hiding place, the crawl space below the house. His face still burned at the thought of the beating. He remembered standing before his parents crying and thinking to himself that it had been only a matter of seconds that he was blind to Yoji. The mourners above began chanting softly beneath the minister's incantations of comfort and ceremony. Tosh squeezed his eyes shut and wished he were dead.

Soon after the observance, life for the Hatanaka family returned to a semblance of normality. Bunjiro took his boat and nets to sea every morning as usual, Tosh played alone in the light of the companion sun, and Atsuko attended to her chores.

One day, she took the round legless *daruma* in hand and filled in one eye with one of Yoji's crayons. As she gazed at the fierce grimace of the ornament's face, she saw or thought she saw the thick eyebrows and the contorted mouth form a smile. She dismissed the idea instantly as a flash of imagination. After her mind cleared, she returned the winking *daruma* to the shelf. It sat smug about some private joke.

On a bright, early spring day, a Mountie came to the door of the Hatanaka cottage accompanied by a small man with thick glasses and a dark suit. The government perceived Etsuji Morii as a community leader and had selected him to assist the Mounties. The Japanese community was appalled at the thought of the Black Dragon boss in cahoots with the *hakujin* authorities, but few protested openly for fear of reprisal. Most shuddered at the kind of deal Morii must have made for his complicity.

Bunjiro glared with contempt at the little Japanese man. Atsuko stood behind her husband.

"The Minister of Justice," the Mountie read aloud from a document, "has on the 5th day of February 1942 ordered that ..."

Morii translated, *"The Minister of Justice says ..."*

"all male Enemy Aliens of the ages of 18 years to 45 years inclusive ..."

"all Japanese men between 18 and 45 ..."

"shall leave the protected area herein before referred to on or before the first day of April 1942 ..."

"Hatanaka-san must report for work detail at a selected road camp ..."

★

"*Otōsan!*" she shrieked in her sleep. She sat up awake. The fatigue of sudden consciousness hit her as she looked around. She soon realised she was at home in her son's basement. All at once she remembered the yearning she felt in her dream.

> *Yoji ... kawaisō ne. His kawaii face – if I could only see it again, to feel him near, to be with him. I bathed him every day and called him yancha-bōzu. He got into everything. Is he there on seven clouds? Floating into mist? Towards the mountains?*

★

Atsuko had not heard from Bunjiro for two months when she received orders to abandon her home and report to Hastings Park in Vancouver. There she and her son were to be detained until "evacuation" to the Interior.

She had heard the rumours about the "Pool," the old Livestock Building of the Hastings Park Exhibition Grounds set up as a clearing house for all Japanese Canadians from outside Vancouver. Men and women were segregated into two huge areas containing rows and rows of bunks. No privacy. Some slept in the horse stalls, cleaned in a perfunctory manner. The toilets had no doors. There was no leaving. The building was guarded twenty-four hours a day.

At least Atsuko and her son stayed together in the same bunk area, but misery still remained their companion. The smell of lime and animal droppings coated their nostrils every moment of their stay. Makeshift blanket walls between bunks made for an insufficient semblance of privacy. The unappetising food, a meagre starchy gruel, caused an epidemic of diarrhoea. Tosh had it for the entire

two weeks they were in the Pool. By the time she received transfer
orders, Atsuko was at her wit's end. She had had little sleep, her
strength had all but left her limbs. At length, word came that she and
her son were to leave Vancouver for an internment camp called
New Denver.

After the Mounties had helped to carry her possessions to the
Canadian Pacific Railroad station, she was interrogated one last
time. Atsuko was spared further indignities through the actions of a
nisei interpreter, Mitzi Abe.

"Do you have any family in Japan?" an older Mountie asked.

Mitzi translated, *"You don't have to answer this one."*

She replied, *"Thank you."*

Mitzi spoke, "None."

A pause and then a smile. As he dismissed her, the Mountie said
"thank you" in Japanese.

★

She rolled over and eyed the ceiling. Her ears pricked up. Something stirred in the darkness. A murmur swelled in the space before
her.

"Who's there?" she called out. "Show yourself."

A sudden laughter sent electric chills through her body. She
pulled herself up and clicked on the light switch. The chuckling
stopped abruptly, but lying on the floor was the winking *daruma*, a
jagged smile clearly visible despite the crack down the middle of its
face. The *daruma*? Laughing? Impossible, she thought. My son is
right, I *am* going senile.

★

Yet another storm threatened in the wind and billowing clouds.
The snow came heavy and wet, clinging to the trees in desperation.
But at night with lanterns hung on boughs, the forest took on a
magical appearance.

Christmas was coming, and Atsuko liked to play at being a

Christian at this time of year. She decorated the humble New Denver shack with homemade streamers, candles and the few ornaments she had saved from her former life. As she danced around the cramped one-room hut, she insisted a Christmas tree was needed to complete the decorations.

"Toshio," she called in Japanese. "Find a Christmas tree for us."

"Speak English! We're in Canada!" he complained. His face turned sour at the thought. "What we got to celebrate anyhow?"

"Please, find tree," she asked in an awkward English.

As he slammed the door, Tosh wrapped away his complaints in his thin cloth coat. About an hour and a half later, he came home with a five-foot fir, full in the middle and deep green. The rest of that evening was spent trimming it. From time to time, she shed a tear for her still lost husband. Tosh played in a corner out of sight.

The days leading to Christmas were the happiest she had experienced since leaving Vancouver Island. Reverend Murata of the United Church persuaded the internees to put on a show on the stage of the Recreation Hall, a roughly hewn building large enough to hold a crowd of a hundred. Everybody threw themselves into the project wholeheartedly. One of the *nisei* organisers thought of arranging for Grace Terakita to come all the way from Slocan City to sing her melodious rendition of "Shina-no Yoru." Fortunately, the B.C. Security commissioners could not object to the request.

Christmas Eve and the Rec Hall was transformed into the Princess Ballroom of downtown Vancouver. "Neat" Mizuyabu, in a refugee tuxedo, was the congenial emcee for the evening. In the wings, the *odori* dancers waited in their salvaged *kimono*. The older *issei* readied themselves for their performance of a classical Japanese tragedy. Grace Terakita smoothed her favourite dress as she waited with her pianist, Vernon Hakkaku, for her cue to step elegantly on stage. Tosh watched from the foot of the stage, lost in the illusion of a show.

Atsuko prepared the tea in one of the nearby shacks. The snow began to fall in swirls and clumps. She thought that later she would have to ask for help in carrying the teapots and confections to the hall. A knock at the door surprised her; she gingerly opened it, thinking it was probably a volunteer. From a curtain of snow stepped a figure white with mystery. She stepped back fearfully. The inner light melted away the obscurity and a warm glow filled her. It was Bunjiro, worry-lined and travel weary.

"Okāsan" was all he said. She placed her hands together in supplication and muttered a Buddhist prayer, but she kept her wet eyes open to prevent her husband from disappearing.

He clasped her hands between his, lowered his head and lightly kissed her knuckles. They both began to cry silently.

★

As she turned off the light, her spirit sank as the darkness of the basement apartment surrounded her. She thought she heard something skitter along the linoleum floor – a surreptitious rodent, perhaps. It seemed to snicker. She buried her head in the pillow.

He had been a good man, she said to herself. He had travelled three days in the back of a pickup truck to rejoin his family. A good man.

So she had thought the day she found him dying in their two-room flat in downtown Toronto. An abundance of money, food and fulfilled dreams had all seemed possible but something would not allow happiness in the Hatanaka household even during the prosperous 1960s.

Atsuko had arrived home after shopping for the weekly groceries to hear a groaning from the adjoining room. She burst open the thin wooden door to find Bunjiro collapsed by the bed.

She lifted his head with her arms and held him closely.

"Forgive me," he begged.

"Nothing to forgive."

"No. No, you must listen."

"Shii," she blew through her lips in an effort to calm him.

"I never told you, I am the second son ..." he coughed ... "the *bastard* second son ..."

She remained calm but silent.

"I agreed to my divorce because Toyama found out ... hokoriga deta ..." He seemed delirious. "My family exiled me to protect me ..."

She suddenly understood her husband: his past, his presence in Canada. She gave him a forgiving smile. A bastard son whose identity is revealed, even in this foreign land, meant shame and ridicule. She lowered his head and called for help. By the time a doctor arrived, Bunjiro was dead.

Second son. Second sons always have the bad luck. My first son, he's grown up, married, has a family ... lost him long ago.

★

She listened to the voices of friends.

"Hatanaka-no obāsan, so sad these days."

"*Ma*, she's always sad."

"Not as much as she is these days."

"Ever since she moved into that basement. You would think a son would have more respect. She must feel awfully embarrassed."

"Ah, sō ne."

"It's that hakujin wife. She is such a horrible woman. Doesn't care about her mother-in-law. Spends all her husband's money."

"I know. She buys Kentucky Fried Chicken at least twice a week. *Oshare ne*! Can't that woman cook him a decent meal? At least for her own daughter's sake?"

★

Her hands clenched into fists as resolve once again filled her. She climbed to the top of the basement stairs, tied one end of the skipping-rope to the door handle, the other end in a knot around her neck. She peered into the gaping chasm below. Her thoughts raced.

For the past two months, she had wandered the open streets of the neighbourhood. Cars slid by along the busy suburban four-lane, indifferent and anonymous. She was always the only one on the sidewalk, her mouth wide open, her eyes bulging, her arms spread apart.

Each time the police found her and brought her home, she explained she was searching for someone she had lost. An exasperated Tosh decided on a nursing home.

"*Okāsan*, you must go," he explained in his professional voice.

"No, I not go," she insisted in broken English.

"You are bordering on senility. I have no choice. You are going."

Atsuko stared at her son a long time before answering in Japanese, "You bring shame to me."

As she stood at the top of the stairs, she knew she was on the brink of discovery. The stillness of the moment was audible.

Her attention was suddenly diverted. Laughter, a mean husky chortle, came from down below. She strained her eyes in an effort to discern the source.

In a swift motion, the *daruma* swooped up from the darkness, its one-eyed, cracked face contorted with demon cruelty. She fell back a moment. The laughter turned to wind and pressed her against the door.

She roared at the top of her lungs, "You! You have always denied me. You will never deny me again." With a great leap, she lunged at the hovering figure and pulled it down into the depths. The skipping-rope snapped taut and held.

★

At the funeral, the gossip flowed unabated. Two *issei* women cackled like parrots in a cage during after-service tea in the basement of the church.

"Toshio-san found his mother with a smile on her face," rattled one, the loose skin of her neck vibrating. "And there was a daruma beside her."

"Sō ka?" said the other while nodding her head.

"I remember seeing that daruma at her house."

"Me too. It was a nice one."

"The second eye was filled in."

"*Ah ra!* Her wish must have come true then." She lifted a cup to fill her mouth with the taste of tea.

Moon Over a Ruined Castle

KOJŌ-NO TSUKI

To rise and fall is people's fate. Shines the moon so bright
Looking down upon the world lying far below.
How sublime the moonlight over the ruined sight.
How I love the moon that shines on the depths of night.

Somewhere in the Slocan Valley, caught in the no man's land between the Selkirk and Purcell mountain ranges, stands a ghost town known as Sandon. Over the years, landslides have squeezed rock and gravel in on the ruins. The sheer height of the surrounding canyon walls allow for only a few short hours of sunlight daily.

Sandon used to be prosperous. Once in support of the silver and lead mining that seemed endless, it boasted twenty hotels and bars, two breweries, a theatre, several brothels and a general store. Saturday night shootouts at the Maple Leaf Saloon over some sleight of hand poker, drunken street brawls till morning and prospectors boasting of sudden wealth were commonplace in the affluent boomtown. Sandon was the wild west until the early part of the 20th century when abruptly the mines were worked out. The prospectors and con artists left, and its dead became ghosts.

Until the 1940s, the town lay in the shadow of isolation. "Don't go there," legend warned. "It is a land of perpetual night, a mere ravine caught between steep mountain precipices, where men dare not breathe, lest their very breath turn to ice." Despite the warning, men, women and children did go, forced to go by an authority that deemed Sandon perfect for its purposes.

★

Kaz Fujibayashi thought the train ride boring. An endless array of mountains rose in the distance like pillars holding up a ceiling of clear blue sky. The evergreens that lined the rail corridor grew thicker with each passing mile. For the freshly scrubbed seventeen-year-old clutching a cardboard box, however, the final destination of the trip meant much more to him than the passing panorama.

Kaz, a short five-foot-two, was nicknamed "Six" as a tease. He possessed keen eyes, a slow drawl and an ambition to learn. Manhood had begun to sculpt his body, but he still had legs too short for his torso and acne scars that marred his face. Despite his "shortcomings", as his friends quipped, he felt very lucky. He was on his way to the University of Alberta which had accepted him into its Agricultural Methodology course of studies. A timely turn of events since the order for Japanese Canadians to evacuate the west coast came down from Ottawa soon thereafter.

He leaned against the window and worried about his mother and little brother. He had no idea what fate awaited them. He knew they were about to be exiled to some camp in the Interior, but to where he could only guess. Certainly his mother didn't know, even as she said her goodbyes to him.

He recalled standing in the cold of the CP Rail terminal within a circle of sunlight shafts. The station was strangely deserted. Most of the trains had already left, taking away the quota of Japanese Canadian internees for that day. He felt more than a little self-conscious about his fortune and his future which resided on a campus in Alberta and not in some lonely ghost town.

His mother was there to bless him with a self-conscious kiss and a *bento* of rice balls and pickled radishes. Chiemi Fujibayashi, her eyes clouded by failing vision, had held onto the hope that her eldest son would be able to support the diminished family of three after her husband's death in a logging accident. She knew education was the only way he could do so. The University of Alberta offered the perfect opportunity despite the fact that she herself was about to be evacuated, separating her from her son even more so and with no guarantee of communication. "Kazu-*chan*, study good. Come back," she whispered in her best broken English. Kazuto bowed slightly and cried quietly at the prospect of never seeing her again.

The image of his mother on the platform beside the long, steaming dragon of a train pulled Kaz away from the window and into thoughts of what he had left behind. Vancouver's patriotic Union Jacks unfurled before him. The Princess and Empire Hotels on East Hastings stirred with raised glasses and arguments about the war. His mother's voice softly humming the haunting melody of

"Kojō-no Tsuki" floated about his ears. Her last words to him surfaced; the Japanese was fluid. "Kazu-chan, don't worry about me
or Mat-chan. Just be a good boy. Somehow we'll be together
again."

Her short, pudgy arms flattened across her chest, her bloated
legs drew tightly together. She began to shrink as the train pulled
away. She weakly raised a hand and waved; her moon face smiled a
horizontal crescent. Kaz waved back bravely.

The tracks clicked, clicked, clicked. Six mindlessly thumbed his
bento box. He hesitated. The smell of home would make him feel
homesick; the smell of Jap food would bring trouble to him. He
concealed the Woodward's cardboard box beneath his seat.

Outside the window, low-lying clouds, snagged on tree tops and
torn apart in the wind's drag, seemed like desperate phantoms. He
rested his forehead on the cool glass and thought about girls to forget his hunger. He wasn't very experienced with them, but he
liked to talk with his pals when they gathered after Buddhist
church service – usually beside the baseball diamond in Powell
Grounds. "Sox" Tanaka was forever bragging.

"Yeah. That Michiko sure likes me," he would say.

"How d'you know?" asked "Lefty" Furutani.

Six injected, "She sure is swell."

"I know 'cause I say so. Okay with you, wiseguy?" Sox flexed
his *judō*-strengthened arm. Lefty backed down.

"She reminds me of some movie star," Six asserted. "Yeah, that's
it! A movie star."

"Hey lover boy," called Sox, "quit dreaming. You ain't got a
chance. Not with your mug."

"Ah, I was just saying how pretty she is."

Lefty offered, "My *otōsan* says a woman's beauty is in the nape of
her neck. The whiter it is, the more beautiful she is."

"What are you, some kind of Jap lover?" asked Sox.

"Hey, what're you saying about my dad? He's a loyal Canadian."

"Ah, give me a break, you dope. All I'm saying is you gotta look
at the gams, the legs! You whistle at her neck and she's gonna think
you're nuts. What a moron!" Sox rapped his knuckles on Lefty's

crew-cut head and then chased him home. Six stayed behind and considered the nape of Michiko's neck ...

The train slowed its pace. Six awoke with a thud against the glass. The train complained as it abruptly stopped. He squinted to get his bearings and saw a sign. "Welcome to Hope" – a friendly gesture, he thought. The boy settled back in his seat, contemplating the hope he and his mother held for Alberta.

He considered the *bento* again. The rice balls would sure taste good just about now. He knew his *okāsan* made them the best.

Two grey men entered the car; identical heavy suits, long coats and stern faces made each indistinguishable from the other, except that one was huskier. Kazuto sank low in his seat trying to be inconspicuous, but the two men headed straight for him.

"Son," began one of the twin officials, "my name's Burton. He's Anderson."

Kaz nodded his greeting.

"Mind if we ask a few questions? Where're you headed?" he asked, not waiting for permission.

"What's your name?" Anderson growled.

Kaz answered quickly, wishing not to offend, "Alberta. Six Fujibayashi."

Anderson looked at Burton. "The call was right. He is one of them."

Burton turned to the boy. "I'm afraid you'll have to come with us, son. Get your things and follow us."

"I don't understand," stammered Kaz, feeling cold in the stomach.

"You don't understand. Right," said Anderson ironically and grabbed the boy roughly by the arm. He breathed heavily into the boy's face. The sour smell was nauseating.

"Take it easy!" Burton said. He whispered in an effort to pacify his partner, "Let me take care of him. You're too drunk." The burly Anderson let go.

Kazuto was shaken but obedient. As he stepped off the train, he looked around. The town of Hope was shrouded in a mist, its moisture beginning to wet his face; he would always remember seeing the town through tears.

Twenty-four hours after Kaz and his mother had parted at the CP Rail terminal, the young teenager found himself standing on the same platform escorted by the two grey men. His education pass hadn't impressed the authorities even though it bore the proper signatures and stamps of approval. "It must be a forgery, some kind of trick," asserted Anderson to his superiors.

Kazuto, identified as an Enemy Alien and a possible fugitive, was going to Sandon, a name unfamiliar to him, but it inspired a cold fear in him and he didn't know why. The boy winced at the oppression implied by the newly coined words, yet he said nothing, not making a move of protest throughout the entire ordeal. In fact, no one suspected anything was wrong with him until it was discovered the young prisoner had caused his wrists to bleed rubbing against the handcuffs.

The air was still. The ceiling high. Seabirds chirped somewhere amongst the cathedral joists above. From time to time, the dragon train hissed steam, impatient to depart. It was already full with internees but had to wait for the okay to take on one special passenger. Kaz kept his head lowered, hiding his identity from curious eyes.

The officials said nothing except for some small talk.

"Cigarette?"

"Yeah, sure."

Kaz snapped his head up and around. Music floated in from seemingly nowhere yet everywhere.

"That's 'Kojō-no Tsuki'," he whispered. A voice sang softly, rising slowly in volume.

> *White frost o'er the autumn camps freezin' all the night.*
> *Flocks of wild geese cry and pass just below the moon.*
> *Where is the moonlight that might have shone so bright,*
> *Shone upon warriors' swords gleaming through the night?*

"*Kāsan!*" he shouted.

"What?" said one official. "What's eating you?"

Kaz abruptly broke away and began running down the platform. "*Kāsan!* Ma! It's me, Kazuto!"

The grey men lunged simultaneously only to miss the stampeding boy by inches. One recovered quickly and sprang to his feet, his heavy worsted coat discarded in the motion.

"Jesus Christ! Get him!" screamed the fallen man.

Three steps later and a shoe-string tackle brought down the escaping youth.

Kaz, the wind knocked out of him, gasped for his mother, his bandaged hands grasping at air. The men dragged him away. The voice faded in the denouement of a minor chord.

Kaz sat dazed, numb from the experience. *Kāsan was there. I know it. I've got to find her*, he resolved silently. The train ride further numbed him. So much so that he didn't complain when he was moved from a hard wicker train seat to the unforgiving bed of a covered truck near Nelson where it was rumoured the townsfolk were waiting with rifles to shoot the "dirty Japs". Fear smouldered in the stomachs of all on the truck even though nothing happened.

Darkness fell early. It was only four o'clock, yet Kaz strained to see his fellow prisoners. An old woman sat hunched over her sleeping granddaughter. Next to her was a middle-aged *obāsan* with thick legs and a full peasant's face. Kaz was the only male.

The steady hum of the truck caused him to fall to dreaming.

> *Mother leaned over her baby, Matsujiro, whose day had been full of a child's activity, as her older son Kazuto slumped into the arms of his love, Michiko. Her soft face smiled as night wind swirled about them. Kazuto lifted his head to see his mother's luminous face rise above the bush, trees and mountains. The moon's shimmer faded in the clear sky above an autumn camp as he awoke.*

Tires hissed as they slid down the grade of the gravel road. The truck ground to a slow pace in the murky darkness. Kaz stirred himself to peer out the back. The road snaked up out of sight; water roared somewhere behind underbrush and forest. Late spring runoff.

Where are we? the boy thought to himself. The women remained still, silence being their only comfort against the unknown.

The truck broke into a clearing and stopped. As he stepped out, Kaz saw before him a crooked river, Main Street a ruin of planks piled in disarray along its banks. Only a remnant of the boardwalk had survived the spring thaw. Extending from the water, buildings lined its curve while several more stood behind in rows. At a far bend in the river with an imposing gorge as background, he noticed a tall building slumped, broken and slightly bent to the wind.

The peasant woman stepped off the truck next. She stared at the sight of the dilapidated ghost town, then lowered herself onto her suitcase before bursting into a cry of anguished Japanese, "Oh God, what a hole! What a hole! Oh God!"

A hand reached out to rest on her shoulder. She snapped her head up to see the gentle beam of a minister's face.

"Okay. Okay. Everything all right," he said in fractured English. "Everyone scare when they first come here."

The woman was soon joined by the others. Kaz stayed at the back of the small crowd, resisting notice.

"I'm Reverend Fujikawa, the camp clergyman," he continued in Japanese. "It's not usual to see people come here by truck. I guess the train can't come today."

The *obāsan* continued sobbing into her hands.

Reverend Haruki "Harry" Fujikawa led them to their quarters. His considerable height, the compassionate look of his eyes and his *kika-nisei* sensibilities made him eminently suitable to his calling. Although born in Vancouver, he had been raised in Japan. His first assignment upon ordination was Canada. After arriving, he decided in order to reach the young he had to speak English and so practised at every opportunity. He brought the plan of action with him to Sandon where many teenaged *nisei* were exiled.

On the way, the minister told the new internees that the camp was specifically for Buddhists. The government in its wisdom deemed them "more Japanese" than members of the United Church. All ministers and their congregations therefore were segre-

gated in order to keep in check their subversive ways. Reverend
Fujikawa's Canadian birth and Japanese education made him especially dangerous.

The women were taken to one of the tar-papered shacks recently built on the edge of town while Kaz was relegated to a
barely renovated building that used to be a hotel. One room with a
few wooden boxes as furniture and a straw-filled mattress as a bed
suddenly became home. Kaz lay down and opened his bloodshot
eyes to the engulfing darkness.

In the weeks that followed, Kaz talked to no one. He preferred
to hear things. There were several camps nearby – Slocan and New
Denver with their satellite encampments of Bay Farm, Popoff and
Roseberry the nearest. Travel was allowed to these places, but
arrangements to do so were difficult. The minister told him about
a makeshift school in town that would be interested in his teaching
ability since he was a high school graduate. Kaz shook his head.
The minister then offered to introduce him to a young woman
who had just finished her degree in social work at UBC. She was
to make Sandon a regular stop on her rounds. Kaz frowned at the
thought of meeting a university graduate.

Most of the time he spent alone. The dreams of his mother
ended with his arrival. Instead, he sweated through the night, often
waking up damp and aching. These bouts with sleeplessness
seemed inexplicable since he otherwise felt no illness.

During the day, his thoughts were pretty much on his mother.
He no longer permitted himself to think about girls. From time to
time though, Sox Tanaka's words came back to him, "You gotta
look at the gams, not at the neck. What are ya, some kind of fruit-
cake? Some kind of Jap lover?" Kazuto felt a rush of blood as he
imagined the pure white sheen of nape in the dip of a *kimono*.

After a few weeks, Kaz took to walking the length of the town
on a daily basis, right to the edge of the forest, the cool darkness of
the trees inviting him inside its seductive interior.

At first, the townsfolk snickered at him. "Young fool. There's no escape. Shikataganai desho ne." After a few days of his meandering, they became alarmed. He began muttering his mother's name with the occasional outburst of anger during his walks. Reverend Fujikawa took it upon himself to talk to the boy after service.

"Is something wrong, Kazuto?" he attempted in English.

The boy remained resolutely silent.

"Is it your *okāsan*? Everyone here worried about someone."

Kaz lowered his head and kicked at the ground.

"I think I can help you. Come with me."

The minister led Kaz out of the church and down Main Street to the tall building at the bend in the river. Inside sat a young woman with permed hair combed up around the edges of a cap. Her long spine pressed her body into a slight downward bend. She smiled to greet her guests; her eyes squeezed tight.

"Shimizu-*san*," greeted the minister, "this is Kazuto Fujibayashi. He new here."

"Kaz, nice to meet you," Shimizu-*san* said as she offered a hand. "I'm new here myself. Been at this only a month."

"Maybe you help him. He worry for his *okāsan*."

"And *otōto*," Kaz blurted out, surprising himself. "Matt."

Reverend Fujikawa smiled. "We find him too," he assured and left the room.

"Now Kaz, sit down. My name is Masako Shimizu, but everyone calls me Rosie."

"They call me Six for short," he said sheepishly.

"Why Six?"

"'Cause I'm short."

Rosie laughed at the answer. Six joined in a moment later.

"Kaz, I mean Six, tell me about your mother."

"Oh she's about that tall and about that wide."

"How old is she?"

"I dunno." He lowered his head.

"When did she come to Canada?"

"Before I was born."

"Okay. Tell me what you like best about her."

"Well, she's a good cook. Miyamoto-*san*, our neighbour, says

she was the best cook up in the logging camps. She makes the best
onigiri. Swell, you know."

"So you lived in a lumber camp."

"Not really. She and *otōsan* worked in the logging camps up until I was born. Then *kāsan* moved us to Powell Street to live in Amitani's rooming house."

"She probably wanted to take proper care of you."

"My brother Matt, too," Six emphasised. "It was all right until
we heard about *otōsan's* accident. He died."

"Oh, I'm so sorry. *Kawaisō ne*."

"After that we just stayed in Vancouver."

"It must've been very hard for your mother."

"I guess so. I know every night she prayed and sometimes cried
to herself. She doesn't know it, but one night I saw her. Her face
was all wet. She was looking up in the sky."

"What was she looking at?"

"The moon, I think."

After she had enough information, Rosie told Six she would do
her best to find his mother and brother. She went to a number of
camps in her travels and saw a great many people. There was a good
chance she would come across them.

Before he left, Six asked, "Are you the social worker?"

"Yes, why?"

"What was university like?" he asked anxiously.

"Well, being on campus was great," she began. "My friends gave
me a lot of support."

"They treat you all right?"

"Yes, but off-campus was a different story. You see, the Security
Commission allowed me to finish my last courses despite the Evacuation. I was virtually the only Japanese left in town by the time I
finished."

The nights that followed were restless ones for Kaz. Every few
hours he awoke, his muscular chest heaving in a cold sweat. His
sleep deprivation became a ritual. He rolled out of bed. Looked

out the window. Wondered at the moon and then withdrew about ten minutes later to go back to sleep. Kaz could not explain his sleeplessness, but somehow he knew he was meant to do something more than lead a somnambulistic existence. There were no voices or visions, just a nagging suspicion.

During the fourth night, the boy was startled awake by an insurmountable urge to leave. His face was flushed, his hands shook and his skin was clammy. He quickly changed his clothes, took the lighted kerosene lamp from the table outside his door and descended the stairs which led to the dark street.

The night air was crisp underneath the curve of stars. Each building face was closed in a death mask. The boy breathlessly made for the forest, a solid wall of darkness with secret passageways revealed in the flickering of the lamp. He chose one with slowly turning mist rising from the ground and escaping between the picket trees. Low sweeping branches scratched his face and tore his clothes. His heart quickened, his eyes stung from sweat. Then he tripped, dropping the lamp which flared and went out. His hands felt for it in a panic, but found nothing. In the still darkness, he heard the chatter of unseen beasts.

Moonlight revealed a small clearing. Kaz couldn't believe his eyes. A castle, a ruined Japanese castle with full moon overhead, stood inexplicably at the far end. The boy hardly stumbled as he headed for its gate.

"What is this? It's gotta be a mirage," he said out loud.

The great wooden gate to the courtyard swung open as though from a push of wind. Inside, a noblewoman stood before Kaz, a cut of smile above a horizon of fan, her *kimono* glistening in the light. Beside her attended an old woman on her knees.

"Who ... who are you?" Kazuto gasped.

The old woman rose and then rushed forward. She bowed before the boy to address him.

"My mistress, the Lady Genyo, welcomes you to her home. Come in and receive her hospitality."

The words were classic Japanese yet Kazuto understood them with no problem. He felt no fear as he walked into the courtyard.

The old woman led him by her cold bony hand. Lady Genyo covered her face and laughed coquettishly. Kazuto followed, confused yet intrigued by all that he saw.

The three continued into the castle proper, into a room with golden *tatami*, a lacquered table and place settings for two. Lady Genyo motioned for her guest to sit. Kazuto knelt gingerly. The old woman disappeared.

"You are Fujibayashi, Kazuto, ne?" Lady Genyo said, facing him.

The boy didn't respond; instead, he marvelled at her powdered round face, shaved eyebrows and red, sliver-thin lips and aura of light. Her long cascade of hair came to a point, fastened by a silver bow halfway down her back. The billowed folds of her *kimono* invited his touch.

"Would you care for some food?" she continued.

"Yeah ... yes I would," he stammered.

Lady Genyo waved a hand, and the old woman reappeared with a tray of delicacies to place before the boy.

Kazuto took in the bowls of hot soup, meat and rice all at once. The surface of the soup percolated with tiny leaping fish, tantalising the hunger pangs of his stomach. The steam of the rice coated his face momentarily before he started to eat.

"I'm sorry there isn't much, but we are all alone here."

Between careful mouthfuls, Kazuto asked, "What is this place? This can't exist. I'm in prison here."

"We are all in prison here," the lady responded with a hint of mystery to her voice.

"What happened? Where did you come from?" he asked.

A fan with a pattern of wind and leaves unfolded across Lady Genyo's face. The old woman moved forward. "This is the house of Genyo. My lady's father was a great warrior during the Gempei War. His downfall and indeed his family's downfall came about because the mongrel dog Kurogane betrayed us. The general died at the battle of Dannoura. My lady and I have been fleeing ever since."

Kazuto tried to shake his mind clear, but the hour of night and the heaviness of the food made him drowsy. "I'm sorry," he murmured, "I have to be going." The old woman drew her elongated sleeves across his face. The room slowly disappeared.

Kazuto half awoke to see that he lay in the lap of Lady Genyo. Her hands were gentle. Her face glowed like the moon. When she noticed he was awake, she rose silently and turned away to loosen her *yukata*. Kazuto's mouth fell open as he caught a glimpse of the whiteness of her neck.

She came to him with a rush of wind. He lifted his head and breathed in the jasmine around her. The ruffles of her *yukata* separated slightly to reveal the opal forms of her breasts. He succumbed and pulled her toward him.

Their lips met with a gentle whisper between them. The forest perfume about her and her liquid eyes urged him on to push aside the garment encumbrances. The skin radiated a light so unusually cool that he hesitated, but the redolence of intimacy drew him on.

Lady Genyo smiled and said, "I will marry you."

The morning cast no shadows. Reverend Fujikawa found Kaz wandering Main Street in a listless fashion. "Kazuto, you okay? Looks like you get no sleep."

"I'm awfully tired," he answered sluggishly.

"What happen to you-*no* clothes? They all ripped, all *boro boro*."

"*Sensei*, I'll talk later. Got to get to bed." Kaz stumbled toward home while the minister watched him with concern.

There would be no answers for Reverend Fujikawa because the boy slept through till night.

About midnight, the winds howled through the rafters of the hotel. Hollow tones formed a melody. Minor notes of a familiar song swirled about Kazuto as he woke suddenly. It was his mother's song.

To rise and fall is people's fate. Shines the moon so bright
Looking down upon the world lying far below.

The boy dressed quickly as he listened. He opened his door and saw the empty space where the lamp had been. Panic seized him a moment. He recovered and ran down the stairs out into the cold air. As if driven by instinct, he made straight for the castle.

The tortured tree branches grabbed at him again, but the distance seemed to be shorter. He soon stood in the courtyard; the music of wind and flying snow blew right through him and rose to a crescendo.

The old woman appeared first with *fue* to her lips. She stopped when she saw him. "You like the song?" she asked with dust in her voice. "It is my mistress's favourite melody."

"This can't be a dream," Kazuto whispered.

"No, my husband, it is not a dream."

Kazuto turned around with a start and met Lady Genyo's eyes. She appeared luminous in the moonlight. "Husband?" he replied.

"You don't remember our wedding night?" she smiled coyly.

The boy fell dumb with the memory. His knees buckled. He slowly closed his eyes in the hope that everything would disappear. A soft hand dispelled such hope when he felt it push him toward the awaiting bedchamber.

Reverend Fujikawa instructed some of his parishioners to take Kaz to a spare bedroom in the church. One of them had found the boy in a heap at the edge of town that morning.

The minister noticed the bruises and tattered clothes, but what disturbed him most was the look of exhaustion that clung to the boy's face. It took much massaging and coaxing to revive him.

"Kazuto. Kazuto. What happen?"

The boy groaned and tried to sit up. The minister eased him back to the supine position. In fragments, Kaz began telling him the whole story.

At first, Reverend Fujikawa stared with disbelief. He is making it all up, he thought to himself. Still, the boy's condition led him to consider another possibility, a possibility that gained credence with every revelation. Fujikawa *sensei* sat with eyes widening and hands slightly shaking. "Kazuto, I think you've been with the dead," he said in Japanese.

"What? Are you nuts?" Six blurted out in his fatigue.

"Gempei War *ne*, 800 years ago," the minister said, switching to English.

"It was?" he said, still not fully comprehending.

"I think Lady Genyo is *yūrei*, ghost."

Six turned over, not wishing to be bothered.

"You must listen. If you go back, they kill you."

The boy asked, face buried in pillow, "How?"

"They will tear you apart," said the minister in a deadly serious tone.

An eerie laugh abruptly reverberated through the splintered walls of the makeshift church. Kaz sat up and grabbed for the minister. "Don't worry," Reverend Fujikawa comforted in Japanese, "I will save you."

The moon rose high above Sandon that night, catching the roof peaks in a pale emptiness. A shaft or two entered Kaz's room, accentuating the kerosene light that aided the minister in his task.

Across the boy's bare back, Reverend Fujikawa carefully drew ideograms with brush and black ink. He worked diligently, chanting as he wrote.

"What're you doing, *sensei*?" Kaz asked, squirming a bit.

"Buddhist *sutra*. It save you from *yūrei*."

Kaz lowered his head. The teenager was still sceptical but just superstitious enough to know something unearthly was happening to him. He closed his eyes and thought about the encounter that was to occur later that night.

Lady Genyo's face flowed around the smile that had formed when she found Kazuto bowing on his knees in the courtyard outside her room.

"Husband, what are you doing? Come in. Come in and lie with your wife."

Kazuto shook as he spoke, "No, I can't. I must stay right here."

"Don't be foolish. Come in," she beckoned.

"No, I can't," he repeated as he buried his head in his arms.

"Come in." The woman slid across the distance between them and hugged Kazuto. An instant later, she recoiled in pain and horror. "What is on your back!" she shrieked with a razor-torn voice. "Let me see your back!"

The boy began muttering the *Nembutsu*. "Namu Amida Butsu. Namu Amida Butsu. Namu Amida Butsu ... "

"Your back!" she shrieked again. The *obāsan* assistant appeared and tore the shirt away with her withered hands to reveal the Buddhist writing that covered every inch of Kazuto's skin.

Lady Genyo cowered at the sight of the ideograms.

The old woman gasped. "You've betrayed my mistress," she accused. "Why?"

Lady Genyo's eyes widened, her voice crackled with anger. "*Chikushō-dō!*" she cursed. Her entire body seemed to simmer with blood and thunder. A storm gathered about her; her *yukata* unfurled. She reached out, the very bones of her hands cracking with the strain. Her hair licked and fluttered like flames in a mad wind. She slowly receded into darkness.

"Why have you done this?" repeated the old woman, shaking. She straightened to her full height, defying the widow's curve of her back.

Wind rushed down corridors, gaining strength before sweeping Kazuto into a spin that he felt hard pressed to stop. He closed his eyes as he continued reciting the *Nembutsu*.

"You ... you are Kurogane!" the old woman resolutely concluded. "Only he could have taken her love to cast it aside in the end."

A chorus of agony swelled into the whirling air. Kazuto covered his ears, but the screams still flooded his head. He himself cried out and fell flat to the floor, before opening his eyes a crack. The old woman burst into flames; her wrinkled mouth wailed a death agony that seared the boy's soul.

In a matter of seconds, the castle walls caught on fire. An army of faces rose, decayed and turned to dust before him. Kazuto sank into unconsciousness, expecting what was surely his death.

He shivered awake, dewdrops spraying in every direction. The clear light of day warmed his ground-chilled body. He ached as he struggled to regain consciousness.

He recognised shapes. The forest clearing was empty, perhaps scorched a bit, he really couldn't tell. There was the pungent smell of burnt wood in the air, but the source was not near.

A dream? The thought seeped into his mind as he gingerly took the first steps back to camp. He dismissed it as he coughed in the stench of smoke and charcoal. His body felt heavy. He measured the significance of the events of the past few nights yet couldn't extract any meaning. He felt himself in a no man's land between reality and dream.

A sudden, indeterminate discomfort swelled within him. His stomach turned sour. The memory of hands pulling at him, tearing at him, brought back the pain. His own hands began tearing at the air before him. He started to run, sobbing as he accelerated. His wobbly legs carried him twenty feet before buckling under. He crumpled to the ground in a dead fall.

Chiemi's face appeared as the moon setting upon the naked and glowing contours of the Lady Genyo. Kazuto screamed as unseen hands tore him apart limb by limb.

"Kazu-chan, okinasai."

The instantly familiar voice filled him with delight. A child's gurgling close by confirmed his situation.

"*Kāsan!*" he said with excitement as he wrapped his arms around the stocky woman. He hugged her tightly until she pulled his arms away in embarrassment. "*Naniyo?*" she complained.

He then realised he was back in his room in Sandon. How didn't matter; his mother and baby brother had returned. "When did you get here? Did Shimizu-*san* bring you here? Where were you?"

The rapid-fire succession of questions was left unanswered as Chiemi busied herself with making some breakfast for her sons. "*Nem-mind*" was all she said.

Kaz looked at his mother curiously. Something had changed. Her legs were no longer bloated. Her eyes were clear and her skin was radiant with health.

"You'll never guess what happened to me," he said as a swelling sense of joy entered his heart.

"Ma ēyo, eat your food," she gently scolded in Japanese.

"But *kāsan*, you just don't know."

"I know you've come back to us, Kazu-chan. My family is together again. That's all that matters."

With the meal done, Kaz lay back on his straw mattress and listened to his mother sing while washing the dishes. His brother Matsujiro played with blocks beside him. He slowly fell asleep with warm memories spinning around him.

"There he is! Thank God." The rush of footsteps and concerned voices woke Kaz abruptly.

"What? What's going on?" the boy asked in a confused voice. "Rosie, is that you?"

"Six, you're all right! *Sensei*, he's with us again!"

"*Ah re. Gūru.* Three day is long enough." Reverend Fujikawa switched to Japanese. "You should have called me instead of going for a walk!"

Six shook his head to clear his mind.

"You don't remember anything, do you Six?" asked Rosie.

The boy said nothing as his answer.

Rosie endeavoured to explain, "Fujikawa *sensei* found you in the forest with a high fever. He took you to his place. You were unconscious for three days."

"Unconscious? But how did I get here?" Six asked as he gestured around his room.

"That's what we want to know," said Rosie. "You disappeared. Did you regain consciousness and walk here?"

"Hey, wait." Six twisted his body. "Where's Matt?"

Rosie steadied him. "Don't worry, he's at my place. I've been taking care of him since I brought him from Slocan two days ago." Rosie's face twitched. "How did you know he was in Sandon?"

"He woke me up with his crying." Six looked up to their baffled faces. "He was with my *kāsan* and me right here," he asserted.

Reverend Fujikawa came forward. "Your *okāsan*?"

"Yeah. I'll get her." Six stood and began calling out for his mother.

Rosie looked at the minister before grabbing the boy by the shoulders. "Six, your mother isn't here."

"Of course she is."

"No, I'm afraid not. She's ... she's dead, Six."

"What?"

"It true, Kazuto," confirmed the minister. "She die of ... of, oh how you say?"

"Diabetes," completed Rosie.

"Diabetes?" Six's face dropped with shock and disbelief.

"She hadn't been to a doctor, had she?" asked Rosie.

"No, couldn't afford one."

"So she didn't know she had diabetes."

"She had heart attack in Slocan, Kazuto," revealed the minister. "She die on way to Kamloops hospital."

"You must have been dreaming about your mother and brother ..."

Six was no longer listening; tears welled. Lady Genyo's gleaming white nape came into his mind. Kazuto rubbed his eyes hard to erase the image, trying to replace it with Michiko, his school yard fantasy, but his face grew wet with the sense of loss he felt. Kaz then saw his *okāsan* kneeling beside him just before he fell asleep after breakfast. Her breath brushed against his cheek. Her mouth opened as if to sing, her favourite song perhaps. But no sound came. A moment later, she began to fade. Deep within himself, he felt something draining away. Then as the minister and social worker helplessly looked on, a haunting melody began to play out of nowhere, and the young *nisei* broke into an uncontrollable sobbing.

Kagami

The scream slashed up the mountain sides. A small muscular man burst out through the door of a slouching cabin at the lower end of the valley town. His broad mouth gasped and spat out fragments of words. His shirt ran with sweat. Two of his fellow carpenters grabbed and held him as his face twitched and his eyes grew wild.

"Goro, what's wrong with you?" shouted Muramoto. Goro shook his head in response. His close-set eyes snapped shut in an attempt to erase whatever horror he had just witnessed. His nostrils snorted with his continued effort to free himself.

"What's the matter with you?" Muramoto repeated.

Goro sucked in more air before blurting out, "*Obakemono!* Ghosts! Ghosts!"

The crew stepped nervously back. An audible moan swelled amongst them. The B.C. Security Commission had appointed Isamu Muramoto to head a group of seven men to go to the ruined and abandoned town to refurbish the decaying shacks and buildings proposed as a wartime measure to house a thousand Japanese. The tall, rugged *bōshin* with keen eyes and full moustache hired men he knew from the logging camps. Each and every man, understandably, had hesitated. There was much talk about Sandon. The obscure settlement lost in the mountains of the Interior was rumoured to be haunted by the ghosts of the savage white men and fallen women of the pioneer era.

Muramoto slapped Goro's agonised face. "Stop it! Stop it! Get a hold of yourself." The boss's usually smooth face with its distinct jawline, flat nose and slitted eyes was creased with impatience and concern. "I think you're just trying to get out of cleaning that cabin!" he said to lighten the moment.

Goro slumped to the wet ground, the air still wheezing through his worn, brownish teeth.

"*Bōshin!*" called Shintani from the cabin's entrance. "I think you'd better see this."

45

The four-room cabin was larger than most, but had seen better days. Inside were the usual furnishings of a settler's home: leg-amputated tables, crippled chairs and cabinets, all dust laden and spider webbed from disuse, nothing extraordinary.

"What's so frightening here?" Muramoto asked as he stepped in.

"Look in the other room."

Muramoto ducked his head through the low doorway to the adjacent room. He gasped. In the middle of the floor, a mirror, a full-length Japanese *kagami*, stood draped in cobwebs, its wooden frame slightly cracked. The convex mirror rested on an ornate lacquered vanity, decorated with gold maple leaves.

Muramoto's knees buckled. He had to steady himself against the door frame before his breathing returned to normal. Once recovered, he turned around to see the nineteen-year-old Shintani standing in the doorway. "What the hell is a kagami doing here?"

"Waiting for us," Shintani breathed as he pushed his thick glasses up the small bridge of his nose.

"Don't give me that."

"Well, where'd it come from? There's nothing else that's Japanese around here!"

"I don't know," Muramoto asserted. "Listen, this thing couldn't have scared Goro that much!" Goro was considered one of the toughest of the crew despite his diminutive stature. He could outwork the best of them.

Outside, Goro drank deeply the cool water offered to him. Calm was beginning to be restored.

Muramoto knelt down and grabbed Goro's arms. "Okay. So what got you going?"

Goro's eyes trembled, his muscles tensed instantly. "The kagami. Didn't you see?"

"So what? Are you a little girl? What's so frightening about a kagami?"

"I ... I saw something in it."

"What? Yourself? I guess I'd be scared too!" Laughter rippled through the cool spring air.

"No. That's just it. It wasn't me. It was ... it was ..."

"Who? Who was it, Goro?"

"A woman. A crying woman."

★

At the beginning of March 1942, six weeks prior to the incident, Reverend Kenji Ikuta had made the arduous trip to Sandon from Vancouver. He had been offered the ghost town for the exclusive use of Japanese Canadian Buddhists, as Greenwood had been for the Catholics, Slocan for the Anglicans and Kaslo for the United Church. The B.C. Security Commission's policy of internment by religion was well on its way.

The young minister and the Buddhist temple's president, Eikichi Kagetsu, had travelled by rail and truck to investigate the site for suitability. As he adjusted his wire-rimmed glasses, he saw from his vantage point the broken line of shacks nearly buried in snow along Carpenter Creek. The mining town had long been worked out. Only its skeleton seemed to remain.

Reverend Ikuta's young eyes set in a round, Buddha-like face were shaded with the wear and tear of worry. He sighed under the weight of his responsibilities. Everything seemed too much for a freshly ordained minister just back from Japan.

"Well, what do you think?" asked Kagetsu in Japanese. He exhaled clouds of steam from beneath his wool cap.

"It'll do." Reverend Ikuta shielded his curved, thin eyes against the sun. "We're gonna lose this sunlight soon."

"Yeah, I hear there's only two hours a day."

"Nothing we can do about that. The place will have to do," he concluded.

The next morning, they were on their way back to Vancouver to hire a work crew to prepare Sandon for habitation.

Isamu Muramoto and his men arrived in the ghost town by early April. Much of the snow had melted but the cool temperatures and high winds played havoc with their efforts to clear the debris from the buildings and shacks. Once they made progress during the following two weeks, the work seemed not so insurmountable. Some of the two-storey hotels still stood, their condition serviceable. The boss thought the Reco Hotel could be used as a school. The boardwalk would be repairable once the surging waters of Carpenter Creek subsided.

The crew sat glumly outside their tents by the river waiting for the rice to boil and dinner to be prepared. They talked in hushed tones about Goro's ghost woman. Darkness rapidly collapsed around them.

"Just like the Kagetsu Logging camps, right men?" said Muramoto in an attempt to divert their attention.

"The pay's not as good," Shintani observed. "But the food's just as bad!"

The cook, a grizzled old man who had gone bust on a claim in Alaska before coming south, ignored the comment and poured hot water into yesterday's pot of *miso shiru*.

"Like that," added Shintani. "He still thins out the leftover soup for an extra meal." He stood up and called in a jocular Japanese. "*Oi*! Old man Kagetsu was cheap, I know, but here the government's paying! Use more miso you bastard."

The cook waved off the complaint and hunched over the thin soup like a troll.

A scream. Heads jerked towards the distance where the sky was still bright with the colour wash of sunlight. They all bounded to their feet and began running towards someone or something thrashing in the distant black water. The body disappeared as they drew closer.

When they reached the bend in the river some fifty feet away, they stopped. Near the shore lay a body, its clothes sopping wet, its bulk rising and falling with the lapping of small waves, lifeless in the shallow water.

Shintani gasped, his slight body shaking as he turned Goro over. The face of the dead man seemed content, without shock or horror.

★

Reverend Ikuta's second trip was at the urgent request of Muramoto, his carpenter crew boss. When he arrived, storm clouds had gathered overhead. Drab piles of broken furniture, the remnants of a long bar and assorted torn clothes lay strewn about the melting snow drifts. Carpenter Creek grumbled through the middle of the town, always threatening to overflow its banks during the spring thaw.

A ripple of uneasiness shook through the minister's hefty build as the group of carpenters encircled him to talk. He heard the river complaining.

"Muramoto, you and your men are making good progress here." Reverend Ikuta spoke in a fluid Japanese. "The first evacuees are due in May. I've just about got them organised." Shintani broke in before Muramoto could respond. "This place isn't fit for the living, sensei! Something strange is going on!" His youthful face broke into a sweat beneath his thick oval glasses.

"Don't listen to him, sensei," Muramoto interrupted in turn. "He's let his imagination run wild."

"What's the trouble here?"

"Goro's dead!" Shintani asserted.

"Goro? How?"

"We don't know. We found him by the river," Muramoto stated.

"Two days after ..." Shintani's words were choked off by his boss's glaring eyes.

"Well? Two days after what?"

Shintani hesitated and looked to Muramoto. Light raindrops splashed on their faces.

The boss relaxed his expression. "Go ahead. Tell him, Shintani!"

"Two days after Goro saw the crying woman in the mirror."

The minister carefully inspected the *kagami*. Even though the light was dim inside the cabin, he could see the quality of the artifact.

"Beautiful inlay work. See how the design flows from the back of the mirror to the tansu below? *Made in Kyoto, 1891* – says so right here."

"Sensei, why is it here?" Shintani asked, his patience worn thin. "I think it's an omen of our deaths."

"Omen?" asked the minister as if marginally distracted from his thoughts.

"Why else would a Japanese mirror be here in this godforsaken place?"

"Take it easy, Shintani-san. There's a simple explanation for this." Reverend Ikuta knew these young, undereducated carpenters were superstitious. The fear in Shintani's face was evident. His features seemed to tighten over the narrow skull of his head.

"Sensei's right," Muramoto interjected. "This probably belonged to a jorō. Wouldn't be surprised if this shack was a jorō-ya in its time." He smoothed back his mass of black hair as he speculated. "This is the lower end of town."

"A prostitute? Why would a Japanese prostitute be up here?"

"Probably came through here on her regular circuit. You know, like a travelling salesman."

"I wouldn't want what she was selling," said Shintani in his naïveté.

"Tell me what happened to Goro," Reverend Ikuta inquired.

Careful to include every detail, the young man related the story. The minister's scepticism mounted with every passing moment. "So, death by drowning," Reverend Ikuta concluded after hearing the tale. "Accident."

"Sō ne." Muramoto nodded his head in agreement.

"No! There's something strange about all this," Shintani said. "The business with the mirror. The look on Goro's face when he first came outta that shack. Sensei, if you could've seen it. It was like he saw a ghost."

Reverend Ikuta considered a moment before concluding. "Unfortunate. Tragic even, but I doubt there were supernatural forces at work here." He breathed in deeply. "Let's see what tomorrow brings."

The young Shintani shivered at the thought.

The moon rose high that night, casting an eerie light over the valley. The cabins, the trees and the trace patches of snow pulled on

shiny coats of black shadow. Only the wild, roaring laughter of
Carpenter Creek could be heard as the men struggled to sleep.

Shintani tossed in his discomfort, yet he was careful not to dis-
turb the others in the tent. At length, the adolescent decided to
arise and venture outside. He stretched to his full height and noticed the sky expanding above him. Even without his glasses, he
could see the avenue of stars sweeping in a gentle curve to infinity.

Somewhere below, he heard the rolling of the water and felt the
pull of the current. He stepped forward gingerly, enjoying the
crunch of ageing ice. There was enough light for him to find his
way to the shack.

Inside, he groped his way into the room with the *kagami*. He
stood before it, squinting to see into its depths. Suddenly a bright-
ness filled the surface. He stepped back startled and turned away.
Before long, he recovered enough to look once again.

Dazzling points of light formed an image in the mirror. Shintani
stared in amazement. It was a woman. A woman dressed in a silk *kimono*, glimmering like gold. It displayed a pattern of tossed maple
leaves.

"Masaru," she whispered. Her lips moved like liquid. The eyes
began as sharp points at the tips and curved fully round the irises,
deep reservoirs of black ink. Her face, stained with tears, shone
pale like the moon in winter. "Masaru," she repeated.

Masaru? It had been a long time since anyone had called him by
his first name. He said nothing.

"Masaru, I knew you'd come in the spring. Help me and I am
yours. Help ..." The voice trailed off into silence.

"No! Don't go! How did you know? How can I help you?
How?" The image faded as darkness filled the room. Confused,
Shintani bolted abruptly out of the shack. Outside, the rumble of
the river drew him to its edge.

At the shoreline, he stood mesmerised by the moonlight on
crystal ice and black water. An aura of light suddenly appeared
above the river. Out from its middle, she appeared to him, her skin
shimmering as in the mirror. The *kimono* fell away. The twin
moons of her breasts heaved to her rapid breathing. The provoca-

tive roundness of her abdomen tapered into her long legs which disappeared into the bright light. Her hair unravelled and swept about her nakedness. She floated just beyond his reach.

"What do you want of me!" shouted Shintani.

"Masaru help me. Help me and I am yours."

Shintani's lips trembled. He inched towards the water. Her voice sounded from farther away. He moved forward to hear.

Behind him, he heard other voices but blocked them out. He had to have her. She began to sink into the water. He lunged, diving after her. The men shouted as they thrashed in the water, making their way with difficulty. His lungs filled. He choked but never dared to raise his head. The shouting grew louder. He saw her slip away in the flow of the stream. Suddenly content, he closed his eyes and drifted after her.

"*Chikushō*!" Muramoto cursed. He pulled Shintani's limp body to the shore. "We were so close. I saw him drowning. He was alive!"

"Muramoto-san, there's nothing we could've done to save him," assured Reverend Ikuta. "I just can't understand why he did it."

"Bakemono," said the cook. "That mirror."

Muramoto's eyes suffused with blood. The corners of his mouth tightened to pull his lips into a mad grin. He bolted and headed straight for the shack. He crashed into the room, picked up a broken chair and smashed the mirror. Some large pieces of silvered surface remained in the frame but most of the glass shattered and rained onto the floor.

The rage in Muramoto subsided like a receding flood. He stood panting for calm. The others in the room witnessed everything in silence and then shuffled out to their tents.

That evening Reverend Ikuta couldn't sleep. He decided to lie near the opening of his tent to breathe in the fresh air. Perhaps then he would finally be able to relax. When he opened the flap, he made out a figure in the distance moving toward the lower part of town.

He rolled out of his sleeping gear and scrambled into the cool, dark night. After a few feet, he stopped. He strained his eyes. Shadows told him there was light but he was hard pressed to see anything. Then he caught sight of something moving into the shack containing the shattered mirror.

The minister cursed and moved quickly. After he entered the cabin, he cupped his ear to a mumbling in the next room. A light emanated. He moved toward it.

From the doorway, Reverend Ikuta saw Muramoto kneeling before the *kagami*; the larger pieces glowed brightly for a moment before dimming.

"Don't go!" the kneeling man said in desperation. "How can I help you? How …?"

"Muramoto!" barked the minister. "What're you doing?" He shook him by the shoulders. Muramoto fell to the ground muttering to himself. His eyes were touched with madness.

Reverend Ikuta tried again but could not bring the boss to his senses. Suddenly, the mirror brightened in intensity once more. He shaded his eyes as he saw the figure of a woman. "Kenji. I knew you would come in the spring. Help me. Help me and I am yours …"

He pulled back. The sudden realisation of drowning filled his being. He closed his eyes and began reciting:

> *Buddham Saranam Gacchami.*
> *I go to the Buddha for guidance.*

> *Dhammam Saranam Gacchami.*
> *I go to the Dharma for guidance.*

> *Sangham Saranam Gacchami.*
> *I go to the Sangha for guidance.*

> *Namu Amida Butsu. Namu Amida Butsu. Namu Amida Butsu.*

The minister stopped chanting when he heard a woman crying. He opened his eyes just as the light faded to a dull glow. In the largest of the mirror fragments knelt a woman with dishevelled hair dressed in muddied clothes. Her torn *kimono* casually opened to her sagging breasts, withered by the weight of age.

"Who ... who are you?"

She looked up. Her small, plain face appeared concave, emphasised by her sunken cheeks. The lips thin and cracked. The chin receding. Her eyes bereft of spirit stared out as if pleading. Her voice was weak, hollow, unearthly. "I am the soul trapped in this mirror by the curse of an uneasy death."

"What were you ... in life, I mean?"

"A low, common jorō. I came here as a picture bride, full of hope, but it turned out to be my downfall."

★

"Are you Suzuki, Yayoi?" asked a gap-toothed small man in a bowler hat. The dock of Vancouver Harbour in 1923 was bustling in the noonday sun. The well-dressed young woman weighed down with luggage could barely hear the intruder.

"Excuse me, I'm waiting for my husband." She looked away to give him the hint.

"Are you Suzuki, Yayoi?" he asked more loudly.

"Yes, I am."

"Then I'm the one you're looking for."

Yayoi gawked in shock at this unctuous little man in a rumpled, ill-fitting suit standing before her. His thin shoulders seemed too slight to hold his chestnut-shaped head. The gap between his front teeth made him into a caricature. He was half her height.

★

"He was not the man who was in the picture I received in Japan. I ran away from him shortly after. I had no choice but to become what I am." She turned her face away. "I was forced to travel around these mountains to service the miners."

"Why do you take men to their death?"

"I do in death what I did in life. I lure men to me, but now I am cursed to watch them die. Such is the karma for the life I lived."

"How … how did you die?"

She faced him and said abruptly, "I need help. Your help." Her eyes flashed with anger. "You are the ones fated to be here. I knew you would come in the spring …"

"What do want from me?" he asked fearfully.

"In Mine-shaft Four, you will find my body. Recover it and bury it properly. The curse will be broken. I will be able to rest forever." With these words, she disappeared, the light extinguished.

The next day when the sun was high and warmed everything it touched, Reverend Ikuta and two of the crew explored Mine-shaft Number Four of the abandoned Slocan Star Mine.

Darkness swallowed the young minister as he inched down the shaft, suspended by a coarse rope. He heard the worried voices of his companions fading as he descended. The two men above were in the light of the cave entrance, standing before the abyss their foolhardy *sensei* had insisted on entering.

Sharp rock walls scratched his hands. The updraft of air swirled dust, and he began to choke. He felt engulfed in darkness and humidity.

He reached bottom with an unexpected thud. In a few moments, the men sent down a lighted kerosene lamp. The light was dull – enough to see the debris of mining but not much else. No corporeal remains.

The minister stopped as he glimpsed a reflection amongst the rubble. He soon dug out two hair combs and a silver hand mirror. The metal was corroded but he could make out writing. "No body. These will have to do," he remarked to himself. He signalled to be lifted up.

"These must have been hers," guessed Reverend Ikuta as he displayed his findings to the gathered crew.

"How do you know?"

"Look at these markings," he said, offering the mirror. The

ideograms for "the third month, the third day" were scratched into the back. "In the old days, the third month was called the Month of Life, *Yayoi*. Spring."

Reverend Ikuta solemnly walked back to camp as he pondered the irony. The day he and Kagetsu had first arrived to survey Sandon was March 3, 1942.

I knew you would come in the spring ... Her voice haunted his ears.

A week later, the minister and five men in plaid workshirts and dungarees huddled together amongst the clump of trees that marked Sandon Cemetery. They watched as the former crew boss, Isamu Muramoto, was helped onto the back of a flat-bed truck — his body huddled like a scared rabbit, his eyes empty. He was headed for the sanatorium at New Denver.

Reverend Ikuta then conducted a service. He stood over a small mound of earth near the remaining headboards. After reciting the proper *sutra*, he lifted his head to speak. "Many have met their fate here in Sandon. Tanizaki, Goro died by drowning," he said gesturing toward a nearby grave. "Some died in snowslides as they walked the trails to work. Others in mine cave-ins. Here lies the only evidence of Suzuki, Yayoi's existence — her beloved mirror and combs. We never found her remains. We can only guess that she fell or was pushed down the mine-shaft. For what reason we shall never know. We can only hope she sought refuge with the Buddha. Having gone to that refuge, she will have been delivered from all pain. Namu Amida Butsu. Namu Amida Butsu. Namu Amida Butsu."

From the late spring through to fall, the Japanese Canadians arrived by rail and truck. Almost a thousand had settled in when *Obon*, the Festival of the Dead, came around at the beginning of August. A parade of children in bright *kimono* danced along the restored Main Street to *minyō* performed by skilled community musicians. The *chigo* led by Reverend Ikuta made its way to the

Buddhist church which had been set up in the old Methodist church. There Reverend Ikuta attended to the *butsudan* and held a service that welcomed back the dead for commemoration.

Duties performed, solace given, the young minister relaxed in bed, contemplating the day's sights and sounds. His mind drifted to the events of last spring, to Yayoi. Gradually an amber light expanded over him from above. He propped himself up. A sensation filled him, like the warm waters of a river caressing him in a steady flow.

"Yayoi? Is that you?"

No answer. No vision. The light receded but the warmth remained. In the closing dark, the minister sat wondering at the rapture of drowning.

Night with Her Train of Stars

Rain fell in wide sheets across Mission Mountain. The water hit his face like a soaked washcloth and flowed down his neck in temporary veins underneath his shirt. He wiped his face clean every few seconds. He felt every curve of skin against bone. His three-day growth of beard scratched the callouses of his palms. The sopping shirt under his oilskin coat sucked at his emaciated body; he shivered involuntarily.

Beneath his feet the long mountain road dissolved to a churning, sliding mud that constantly sucked at his feet, threatening every step.

Distant flares of lightning revealed the sawmill at the end of the road. It cowered like some black hulk beneath the great envelope of storm. He was almost there he guessed. Another hundred yards or so.

His eyes throbbing with the blood of punctured veins strained to find a clear pathway through the oozing mud of the road. The wind drove the water like darts.

He next made a false step and fell on his back, landing with an uncomfortable splat. He hastily tried to recover, but the mud rushed around his hands, pulling him in deeper. All he could do was to roll over onto his stomach. His neck strained against the weight of his head as he lifted his face upwards. He shielded his eyes with one muddy hand freed with great effort.

A lightning bolt cracked above him sizzling the upper branches of two trees by the shoulder of the road. With the explosion came the yawn of branch and root. The force propelled the evergreens across the road, just missing him. They teetered for a moment before plummeting into the darkness beyond.

His face contorted by terror, he couldn't believe the sight before him. He crawled to the edge of the cliff and peered into the chasm.

The rain thundered in his ears.

★

The Minto Hotel. "Big Bill" Davidson had built the two-storey, double-winged hotel with painted wood siding, coloured stucco and a shingled roof during the early 1930s. Every room featured running water and electricity. The building itself became the centrepiece of Davidson's dream: an idyllic mining town nestled in the middle of the Bridge River Valley, about 140 miles from the B.C. coast.

The mine had been worked out by 1942, and Big Bill's hotel was empty, the dream dead.

With the Japanese internment, Bill leased his holdings to the government and the remaining townsfolk fled Minto leaving completely usable furniture and cooking utensils behind. They must have imagined the keen edge of a sword next to their throats.

Because of the storm, the lobby of the Minto Hotel was busier than usual that night. Many of the internees had gathered to pass the time honing their card and pool skills. The place was comfortable enough but it was a mere shadow of itself with its faded wallpaper and broken mirrors.

Tadashi Yoshida took careful aim at the two-ball combination shot he was about to execute across the balding green felt pool table. His young challenger and constant companion, Minoru "Crazy" Shimizu, looked on with nervous anticipation. Tad, his hair combed back off his angular handsome face, exuded confidence like a pro at the height of his game. With one smooth stroke, the cue ball caromed off its target and struck the eight ball into the corner pocket.

"*Baka!*" cursed Crazy. "I was sure you couldn't get that!"

"Like it had eyes, pal. Like it had eyes," Tad gloated in the easy slang of adolescent English.

"Okay, wiseguy. That's quits for me," Crazy declared.

"C'mon. One more game," called Tad.

"Nah. It's nearly closin' time anyway."

The lobby's double door burst open with a surge of wind and rain. In stepped a creature of dripping mud and matted hair. He fell to the floor exhausted and mouthing gibberish.

"Jiro!" The *issei* loggers and fishermen began to curse the prostrated and shivering man. "Drunk again! What the hell happened to him? He looks like he's seen a ghost." Shouts and whispers in Japanese rushed around the room.

Jiro, the town drunk, had been in many a sorry state since arriving months before from Vancouver, but he had never been so agitated. His troubles began with his forced removal from the coast via the Union Steamship Company boat to Squamish. During the six-hour train ride that followed, he bitterly voiced his opinion of the government. His fellow travellers slid quietly away from him. After spending an uneasy night sleeping on the hard seat of the railroad coach just outside the small village of Bridge River, he screamed about injustice as he boarded the back of a Neal Evans Transportation truck. The last leg of the journey became a palpable hell with the heat, dust and Jiro's protestations. There was no end to his complaints. The internees were actually relieved when he found alcohol in town – bootlegged from a hidden still, they guessed.

A presence broke through the crowd. The enigmatic Etsuji Morii, a short man with a pencil-thin moustache and bulging shoulders, had controlled Vancouver's Little Tokyo, according to rumour, through blackmail and extortion. His *judō dōjō* was also said to have supplied much of the muscle needed to convince his victims to co-operate. No one knew the truth; no one had ever dared to complain.

With the war came Morii's biggest deal. He helped the RCMP round up Japanese nationals for imprisonment in exchange for Minto, a self-sustaining internment camp – for his own use.

Morii grabbed Jiro by the collar and gripped hard. The mud squirted through his fingers. "Bakayaro! What's the idea of coming in here like this?" He slapped the side of the head. A laugh ruffled through the crowd as Jiro crossed his arms above his head to protect himself.

"Oyabun, please forgive me. I ... I ... I saw ..."

"I ... I ... I," mocked Morii eliciting more laughter. "What did you see? Your own ugly face?"

A sustained guffaw.

"No. No, listen. I saw evil."

A momentary silence settled over everyone. Morii let Jiro go and stood back. "What's that? Evil?"

"I was up on Mission Mountain road ..."

"What the hell were you doing up there?" said a voice from the back.

"I ... I was on my way to Minto Mill when lightning bolts hit two trees. They came to life and attacked me ... nearly dragged me across the road, but I got away ... like bakemono. They jumped down the mountainside."

Bakemono. Monsters. Each man stood still, his skin tingling at the thought. Morii grimaced and squeezed his eyes thin. "What were you doing up on that road?"

"On a night like this?" called another.

"I was on my way to the sawmill."

"Why?"

"Because ..." Jiro searched for an answer.

Morii interrupted, "Because that's where your koji is. You had a taste for sake so you braved this foul weather for a bottle of your own dobuzake." He turned to address the crowd. "He probably saw all kinds of things after he got drunk."

Laughter broke the tension.

"No. No," Jiro pleaded. "I was on my way *to* my koji ..."

"So, you admit to making sake up there!" Morii gestured to his minions. "Tomorrow, we go and break everything up. Can't have such a temptation for the young around here," he said, pointing to the youngsters by the pool table.

"It was evil. Something evil is coming ..." Jiro's words faded away as the onlookers returned to their tables. Soon men riffled cards, broke Boston balls and whispered to one another in discreet conversation.

"Did you see that?" asked an astonished Crazy Shimizu. "Old man Morii really gave it to him!"

Tad scoffed. "Easy for Morii to pick on that guy."

Crazy, pimple-faced and shorter than Tad, decided to take advantage of the boast. "Oh, I suppose you could've handled him?"

"Who? Morii? Yeah, cinch. But I wouldn'ta come in here with such a crazy story. That's just asking for it."

"Do you think it's true, any of it?" asked Crazy as he rubbed his cue against his face.

Tad just looked sideways at the question.

Crazy grinned. An idea shone through his eyes. "Hey, let's you and me go up there tomorrow and see what happened."

"What? What a waste of time," asserted Tad.

"You got something better to do?"

Tad twisted his well-developed torso in an effort to stretch out the kinks before answering. "*Okay we go*," he said mocking a Japanese accent. "One last game?"

"Okay," agreed Crazy as he picked at a pimple.

"See, I told you this was a waste of time," complained Tad as the two adolescents struggled up the road that was still shifting with the mud. All around them, trees sweated with rain in the aftermath of the storm.

"Pipe down, will ya? Keep your eyes peeled," ordered Crazy.

"Eyes peeled for what?" Tad retorted.

"I don't know. Maybe look for evidence of lightning?"

Tad laughed and patted his friend's shoulder. "Good idea, bright boy."

Around the next bend, they found the unmistakable evidence of upheaval. Tree limbs split and bent reached limply toward the ground. Some trees still stood even though their trunks leaned at a precarious angle with roots exposed to the air. There were two obvious craters gaping in front of the boys, as they surveyed the damage.

"Je-sus," Crazy exclaimed, "Jiro was telling the truth."

"About the lightning anyway."

As they looked over the edge of the road, their eyes widened at the sight of two tree trunks wedged among boulders protruding from the side of the mountain about halfway to the base – another 200 feet or so.

"See, Jiro was telling the truth."

"Okay, so lightning struck a couple of trees and knocked them over the side," conceded Tad. "But *bakemono*? There was no evil. Come on. The guy was drunk."

"What's that?" said Crazy, alerted by the sound of machinery. "Quick, hide." A swift shuffle of feet and the two dove behind the safety of underbrush. They looked up to see an automobile headed their way.

The three men, two in the front and one in the rear seat, talked to each other in a jocular manner. The roar of the vehicle was slightly louder than their voices. The man in the back was obviously the boss with his patronising demeanour.

After the worn but functional '29 Nash disappeared around a curve in the road, the boys stood up.

"Say, that was old man Morii!" exclaimed Crazy.

Tad snapped, "Who else would it be? He's got the only car in town. Besides, he said he'd be up here. Look who he had with him – Tanaka and Moriyama, his main *judō* henchmen." The boys followed the muddy tire tracks around the bend and observed the car heading for the sawmill. "Yeah, they're up to something."

"How do you know?"

"You think he'd waste his time coming up here because Jiro saw ghosts? No, there's something in it for him."

"Yeah, let's go see what's what," Crazy enjoined.

From a vantage point above the sawmill, the boys observed Morii and his gangsters with great interest. Andy Devine's mill was deserted because it was Sunday, but the quiet was disturbed as the three men rooted about looking for bounty.

"Tanaka, are you sure Jiro said it was here?" shouted Morii in a gruff Japanese.

"Yeah. It didn't take much to get it out of him."

"One good arm twist," the burly Moriyama added, "and he was only too willing to talk."

"Look!" exclaimed Tanaka. "Here it is." His close-set eyes squinted as he entered a dark, little-used shack away from the mill's main operation.

"Tad," Crazy whispered, "we better get outta here. I don't like what's going on."

"Not until we *see* what's going on," he smiled to reassure his trembling friend. Tad instructed Crazy to wait for him as he sneaked down the hill to the shack's only window. Inside, he saw the men congratulating each other for what they had discovered.

"That Jiro, he's one smart bugger!" Tanaka proclaimed while salivating over the cache of bottles.

"Probably comes up here on the weekend when no one's around to make the sake," Morii speculated.

"There must be twenty bottles of the stuff!" Tanaka exclaimed.

Morii picked one up and examined it closely. "Yoshi. We can take these back and sell them to our friends. There's been a need for some good sake. It's our civic duty!"

The three laughed heartily – the signal for Tad to retreat to his former position up the hill. He soon informed his friend about what was going on below.

Crazy was aghast. He curled his body closer to ground. "Je-sus, how did Jiro manage to make that stuff right under the mill boss's nose?"

"Hey you know Devine hardly ever comes up from Lillooet. Jiro probably gives him a bottle or two when he's here to check on things," Tad suggested. "So why should he care?"

Crazy speculated, "What do you think Morii will do with the stash now? Break it up like he said last night?"

"Sure. You got all that high-school education and you still can't think straight, can you?" Tad admonished. "Shut up a minute, Morii's come outside."

"Hurry up and load those bottles," Morii called to his henchmen. "This'll make a good start."

"Hey, he plans to keep the operation going," Crazy concluded.

"Surprise, surprise," Tad mocked, tapping his friend's forehead. "He'll probably make good money."

In a few minutes, Tanaka and Moriyama filled the trunk of the Nash with the illicit alcohol. The three then boarded the old puddle jumper, started it and drove off down the road back to Minto proper.

Crazy stood up in the safety of solitude. "Say, do you think we could get in on the action?"

Tad turned quickly, "Are you nuts? You know who we're dealing with here? Morii! The Black Dragon!"

"Aw c'mon," encouraged Crazy. "We could sneak a couple of bottles. They'd never miss 'em."

Tad gave his friend a sceptical look.

"Hey," Crazy continued, "you even said you could take him."

"Listen, you ever heard about the Yamamoto murder case?"

"You mean the one on Alexander Street?" Crazy asked. "I heard it was in self-defence."

"Self-defence, my eye!" Tad said. "Morii killed a seventeen-year-old kid. How could that be in self-defence?"

★

In a grim house in the three-hundred block of Alexander Street, Vancouver, Etsuji Morii sat behind his expensive oak desk in his second-floor office overlooking the street. The stars outside offered little light. In the shadows, Morii traded jokes with his minions, the grim Tanaka with his face in a permanent scowl and the huge and ominous Moriyama.

In the middle of a laugh, a boy entered holding forth a fist full of money. He breathed heavily as he wiped the sweat from his brow. There was defiance in his narrow eyes, anger on his lips.

"I'm here to pay my father's gambling debt," he said, as he tossed the money across the desk.

Moriyama and Tanaka moved quickly, almost automatically, to heel this impudent puppy. Morii raised his hand to stop them. He smiled, exposing his copious yellow teeth.

"Yamamoto-san, you're a good boy to do your father's bidding.

Come here and shake hands as a gesture of good faith." He held out a stubby palm.

Out of the corner of his eye, the boy caught a glimpse of Tanaka grinning. "No," he said. "I will not touch the dirty hand of a dog." He turned quickly and ran to the door. "*Saibashi!*"

Morii's tolerance evaporated. He leaped to his feet and gave chase so quickly he left his henchmen behind. Down the stairs in darkness, past the watchman on the front door, out onto the street and heading east, Morii scrambled after the upstart.

By the next block, the *oyabun* took hold of Yamamoto by the back of the shirt and began to administer loud slaps to the boy's head. Yamamoto tried to defend himself by countering with a strong blow to Morii's face. The *judō* master instinctively grabbed hold of the arm and flipped the body to the ground. An audible crack was heard. By the time Tanaka and Moriyama reached the scene, the seventeen-year-old Yamamoto was dead.

★

The autumn rain returned but no one knew it that night in the Minto Hotel. From upstairs in the old building came the sounds of laughter, high-pitched squeals, glasses breaking and good-natured cursing.

"They're having a hot time up there," Crazy declared. The two had gathered as usual to play pool, but the noise and the events of the day were distracting. "Listen to that, Tad. We could be having us such a time if you weren't so chicken."

"Hey, didn't my story about Morii mean anything to you?"

"Ah, nuts to you. You made it up!"

"No I didn't."

"Were you there?"

"No, but I heard about it."

"You heard? Yeah, well I heard the kid stole Morii's car and ran it into a ditch. Morii just wanted an apology and money for the damage done. The kid attacked him and Morii defended himself. The kid got what was coming to him," insisted Crazy.

"And you believe that story? Tanaka and Moriyama told that to the cops so their boss wouldn't have to take the rap."

"Hey, the man got off, didn't he? So what do you say? We could make some real dough here selling a few bottles of booze."

"Je-sus, what do you need money here for?" Tad retorted. "We're in the middle of nowhere. Nothing to do. Nowhere to go."

Crazy stood back. "My old man just got told he lost his store back home. The Custodian's gonna sell it right from under us. We need money. Who knows where we're going to next!"

Tad bowed his head. "The *sake* is evil."

"What?" Crazy shook his head at the subject shift.

"Jiro was right. He saw evil. Something's gonna happen."

A loud crash came from up the stairs. No one dared to investigate.

Night with her train of stars … The poem fragment ran through Tad's mind as he gazed with half-closed eyes toward the clearing sky, through the widening gaps of cloud to the pinlight stars above. Try as he might, he couldn't remember any more of the poem he was forced to memorise in high school back in Vancouver.

He and his parents had made the long journey to Minto six months after the outbreak of the war. His father foresaw all kinds of trouble and so sold the family hardware business to a *hakujin* friend. Yoshida-*san* then went to Shigeru Noma, head of the self-supporting evacuation group, and applied for Minto. All that was required was $1500 in savings to ensure self-reliance, and a little tribute money to Morii himself.

Minto was pleasant enough. Electricity, indoor plumbing and running water piped in from a mountain stream. The Yoshidas lived in a clean three-room apartment above the general store. Still they knew they were prisoners. The Security Commission had warned everyone not to cross the town boundaries, or they would be shot.

"Maybe Crazy's right," Tad murmured to himself. "We oughta skim off some of what Morii's making on Jiro's *sake*. I got nothing for the future. Maybe I could go to university with the money. Hitch up to those stars. But if he ever found out ..."

Tad turned away from the window and surveyed his room of simple furniture and books. He considered where to look for the poem. Might be in *World Poetry In English*, he thought. Aw, who am I kidding? I'm a Jap for Christ sake! I've got as much chance of going to university as I've got reaching them stars.

He pulled the chain to turn on the overhead light. It burned for a second before it flashed blue and faded into black. The next moment, the light in the front room flashed out.

"Funny," he said as he fiddled with the living-room lamp switch. "Both lights blowing like that." A coincidence, nothing to wake mom and dad for. He went to bed, deciding to change the bulbs in the morning.

Around noon, Crazy Shimizu came running pell-mell down the main drag of town.

"Whoa! Crazy, what's the matter? You look like a ghost's chasing you!" Tad said after he stopped his agitated friend.

"Tad, you won't ... you won't believe what's happened!" he screamed as he gulped for air.

"What?"

"One of Devine's trucks went over the side up on Mission Mountain."

"Where on Mission Mountain?" he asked, feeling a bit ill at ease.

"Near Minto Mill."

"You mean ..."

"Yeah, exactly where Jiro saw the *bakemono* trees. Where we were yesterday."

As the day wore on, the facts of the accident came to light. The mill's twelve-man morning crew had headed for work in two trucks as usual. However, one of the drivers, a man named Juntaro, was suffering from a debilitating hangover. About half-way up the road, he passed out, swerved to the right and sent the truck crashing down the side of the mountain. One worker, Minamide, died instantly and another, Takehara, sustained a head injury and crushed ribs. Miraculously, no one else was hurt, not even Juntaro. The truck's fall was broken by two tree trunks which were wedged among boulders – Jiro's *bakemono* trees.

"Something evil has happened," whispered Crazy into Tad's ear as they solemnly stood among the crowd of mourners by the river where the cremation was taking place. The noon-day sun gave off a weak warmth.

"What're you talking about?"

"I heard that lights burned out all over town the night before the accident."

Three men piled wood high around Minamide's linen-wrapped body. A *bonsan* from Lillooet chanted the funeral rites sombrely. One of the men poured gasoline over the pile. Another touched the wood with a torch. The pyre blazed with a great roar, the heat massaging the faces of the mourners.

"Something evil? Nah, evil didn't kill Minamide, and evil didn't save that crew," Tad insisted. "Jiro's *sake* and Morii did it. If it wasn't ..."

Tad suddenly stopped his discourse, diverted by an unusual sound. As the pyre burned, a man reeking of alcohol knelt in front of Minamide's veiled widow, grabbing at the bottom of her long black dress. "Forgive me! Please, forgive me!" he blubbered in Japanese. All averted their eyes. The driver of the ill-fated truck fell to the ground as the widow withdrew from the scene.

The afternoon shadows lengthened, the crowd diminished. After the service, the three men who had built the pyre and stoked the fire now worked meticulously with long cooking chopsticks to pick out the bones in the ashes. They passed the remains carefully from one set of utensils to another for collection and veneration. The *bonsan* chanted over them. A young boy observed the men from a distance. Even farther away, Tad and Crazy sat sheltered among bushes.

The embers glowed well into evening, even after the minister had led the boy away, even after the crew of three had finished their chore and left for home, even as the two continued to watch.

"Tad, let's get outta here," Crazy suggested as he pulled his arms around himself. "I feel a little chilly. Besides, this place gives me the creeps."

"Why don't you go closer to the fire?" suggested Tad, smiling to himself.

"Je-sus, that's what's giving me the creeps!" Crazy jerked with fear at each intermittent crackle and flare. "Look how it glows. There's a lot of phosphorous in these parts. Probably why the fire's lasted so long."

"I think it's the *hinotama* getting ready," Tad replied.

"The what? A *hino*-what?" Crazy asked.

"A *hinotama*. My *otōsan* said when the body dies, the spirit comes out of the body like a fireball and shoots up to *Nirvana*."

"Is that why we're here?" Crazy complained. "To see some fire-ball fly through the sky?"

"Yeah, don't you think that'll be something to see?"

"Je-sus, you believe that hooey? I'd rather be playing pool!"

The ground beneath them quivered. A dull roar broke the silence of the night.

"Holy mackerel, what was that?" Crazy exclaimed.

The ground shook. The roar grew in intensity.

Crazy stood up and shouted. "Let's cut out." Tad grabbed his friend and held him in place.

Suddenly, an explosion burst the pile of burning wood. Charred debris flew in every direction. Smoke climbed upwards in a single, cinder-filled column. From its middle erupted a ball of fire that soared for a moment before arcing across the night sky. The light illuminated the entire valley.

The youths immediately ran in the direction taken by the meteor. As they gave chase, they heard a distant explosion. By the time they reached the settlement area, they saw the roof of a large house on fire. Morii's house.

★

Etsuji Morii sat with legs akimbo in an overstuffed chair, a favourite hauled all the way from Vancouver. With sullen eyes, he scanned the last issue of the *Tairiku Nippo*, a Japanese-language newspaper closed at the outbreak of war. He played with his thin moustache as he read.

A crash and blast tore the paper from his hands and hurled him against the wall. He looked up in horror. The ceiling caved in as a column of fire breathed and consumed the air.

He screamed for help, but the roar of combustion drowned out his panic. His eyes widened as he looked into the inferno.

The myriad colours melded into a face emerging, a face split with a grin from ear to ear. The mouth opened and fiery arms reached forward.

Morii screamed again and spun away, shielding his face from the engulfing tide.

★

Men ran in several directions. Orders for buckets of water rang in the air. Women huddled with their children in front of their cabins.

"Je-sus!" Crazy said. "That ... that thing crashed right into Morii's house!"

In front, just beyond the white picket fence that surrounded the tidy structure, Morii cowered with his minions, Tanaka and Moriyama. His face was white as if sheared by the very flames that were now consuming his home.

"I saw him! I saw him!" Morii cried out.

Moriyama's hands steadied him. "Saw who? Oyabun, saw who?"

"Minamide! He was standing there in the fire after the roof fell in!"

"Minamide? But he's dead, boss. He's dead!" repeated Moriyama.

Tad Yoshida and Crazy Shimizu sat in the lobby of the Minto Hotel a week later, too uninspired to play pool. A cigarette burned at the ends of Tad's fingers, its smoke curling in dead air. The ashes, left unattended, lazily fell to the wood floor.

"You going to Morii's unveiling?" asked Crazy.

"Nah, seen one shrine, you seen 'em all," Tad replied.

"Who woulda figured?" Crazy said. "Morii, religious?"

"Well, after what happened, wouldn't you?" Tad asked.

"So you think it really was a *hinotama*? Minamide's *hinotama*?" Tad drew on his cigarette and said nothing.

Crazy rubbed his face in circles. "I heard Morii saw Minamide standing right in the middle of the fire. Right in front of him!"

"With a devil's smile on his face," Tad added matter of factly. He drew one leg up to his chair and said, "Well I hope Minamide can rest easy now. The *sake's* gone. Minamide's widow and kids are taken care of, and even Jiro's on the mend."

"Yeah, Morii is really making amends," Crazy concluded. "So do you think it was or wasn't?"

Tad looked through the window to the wide expanse of black sky. The avenue of stars pulled away from him, leaving him behind, alone and forgotten.

"Hey, you listening to me?"

"Sorry. What did you say?"

"Do you think it was a real *hinotama*?"

"Oh, I dunno. Might've been."

"Why do you say that?"

"Cause we ain't got much else." *Night with her train of stars* ..., he recalled as he drew on the last of his cigarette.

Night with Her Great Gift of Sleep

Asao Takehara stood solemnly at a distance from the smouldering remains of the funeral pyre. The sun, positioned in the slant of afternoon, gave off a cool warmth, the typical paradox of an autumn day. His well-worn Buster Browns alternately kicked at the ground or nervously worried the burrs of the shoe leather skin. He was small for his age, but his serious face made him appear determined to make something of himself. Just what that fate was to be was unfathomable given his present circumstances. At the moment, his downcast eyes randomly surveyed the ground around his busy feet. Occasionally, he lifted his slight head. His curved, soft jaw tightened. His eyes grew round, wide open to the scene before him.

Three men manipulated crude, elongated *hashi*, cooking chopsticks, carefully sifting through the ashes. As they laboured, they kicked up a cloud of debris, inhaling dust with every breath they took. They choked and spit as they hunched over, grunting with the effort of passing bones from chopstick to chopstick. They conversed in a coarse Japanese. A *bonsan* stood nearby, reciting Japanese scripture through the cloud and smoke.

★

Asao had experienced much in the ten years since his birth on a logging raft near Alert Bay, Vancouver Island. During the first five years, he had nearly drowned three times. It was so easy for a toddler to slip through the planks of the raft into the cold waters of Queen Charlotte Strait.

Fortunately, his mother, Tazuko, was vigilant in watching for such mishaps. Living on a floating log camp was no way to raise a child, Tazuko thought over and over. It was after the third near-drowning incident that she finally decided enough was enough. Her diminutive stature, sloping shoulders, oval face and tender eyes belied a fierce will.

"Why do you want to leave me?" her husband demanded in Japanese.

"It's not safe here. Something terrible will happen to Asao-chan if we stay."

"Ah," scoffed Gunjiro. "You worry too much. He's weak because of your worry."

Asao stood behind a makeshift cupboard, his body flinching with every shout.

"Gunjiro, it's not safe here," she repeated. "We're leaving." She stared in defiance.

Within a week, Tazuko and her son began the long journey to resettle in Vancouver. Taking in sewing and laundry allowed her to make ends meet until she received her husband's contribution – about twenty-five dollars a month. Gunjiro, in the meantime, stayed in the camp until the off-season when he could rejoin his family. He reasoned that since his muscle-heavy body was used to the rigours of logging and wilderness life he would stay where there was a steady job.

Asao enjoyed life on Powell Street in the heart of Little Tokyo. The congested city stood in stark contrast to life on a raft surrounded by choppy water. Tree-dense mountains towered in the distance but they might as well have been faraway lands dreamed about but never explored.

The one-room apartment in Amitani's Boarding House contained a bed with a slumping mattress, a hot plate and a scarred chest of drawers. It wasn't much but it was home. Asao enjoyed the warmth of being near his mother as she ironed neighbours' clothes to earn extra money.

"Asao-chan, you're in the way here," Tazuko complained. Her face grimaced in pain. "Go out and play with your friends." Any irritation aggravated her chronic stomach problem.

Asao looked away and nodded his head to comply. He couldn't look at her to betray the fact that he hadn't any friends. He kept to himself most of the time, preferring books over playmates. The young boy found passageways to adventure in Little Tokyo's alleys and narrow streets. In his imagination, fiery dragons confronted him in dark laneways that led to *mochi* factories and *furōba* establishments. The rough gaming houses presented him with wizened old sailors arguing over tall tales about exotic food and buried treasure.

A favourite pastime was to watch from the shores of Burrard Inlet the ships setting out to sea. He marvelled at how easily they glided through the water. Could they withstand the huge waves whipped up by mighty storms that awaited hapless boats? He thought the crews must be awfully brave to stand against such elements.

The brisk winter winds of early 1942 carried whispers that were sinister and foreboding.

"Asao-chan," his mother said in a hushed sibilant voice, "you can't go to Japanese school after school today."

Happy at not having to endure Tokuda *sensei's* boring lesson and stinging strap, he almost cheered. The worry on his mother's face quickly choked off such elation. "Why not, kāsan?" he asked.

"Nem mind. Come home!" she barked in broken English.

The startled boy looked away.

A few days later, curiosity got the better of Asao. He walked home past the Japanese Language School on Alexander Street south of the docks. The two-storey building had never been welcoming with its slate grey paint and shuttered windows, but that day, the place was ominously silent, the doors boarded against entry.

He took another detour and walked past other places to find they were similarly closed. The *Tairiku Nippo* and the *Minshu* newspaper offices stood deserted and locked.

The whispers grew louder. Something called a *curfew* was mouthed beneath the breath of frightened children. Rumours circulated about fathers disappearing into thin air.

One day, the money stopped coming from *otōsan*. Asao sensed something was wrong when his mother began reading his father's old letters to him in bed.

"Kāsan, where's otōsan?"

"Far away. Far away," she said in a forlorn voice.

"Will we see him again?"

She began to cry. Asao didn't understand and could not do anything except seek her arms for comfort.

Soon thereafter, he heard everyone everywhere saying a word he had never heard before. Young men huddled in groups on street corners cursed it. Women fretted about it. His mother's friends argued about it over tea.

"Kāsan? What is Idō?" Asao asked finally.

Tazuko said nothing at first. Her lower lip trembling, she hugged her son tightly and whispered, "We have to go."

The forced exile to the Interior began with a four-hour boat ride from Vancouver to Squamish. Tazuko carried as much of the 150 pounds of allowed belongings as possible. "Otōsan, where are you? I need you!" she cursed. Asao too worried about his father's fate but said nothing as he dragged a suitcase to the gangway.

Seagulls mocked them as they and several other Japanese Canadian mothers and children struggled on board. Asao noticed the absence of fathers amongst the families. For him, the prospect of a sea journey had lost its allure. The anticipation of imaginary pirate warships and sea monsters faded into the reality of a dark future with a lost father.

When everyone transferred to the P.G.E. Railway train that awaited them at Squamish, Tazuko gave thanks as the unsteadiness of water gave way to the gentle clicking of tracks. The sea voyage had only intensified her nausea and constant stomach-ache. Fortunately, the train ride dulled the pain somewhat, and so she was able to bear the rest of the journey.

About a hundred miles through high timber country at the village of Bridge River, a B.C. Security commissioner with cold blue eyes and thick beard climbed on board. "All right. All right. You're bedding down here for the night," he said.

Those that spoke English translated. Cries of complaint responded, "Where're we gonna sleep? There's no beds here."

"Right where you're sitting. Good enough for you Japs," he growled.

The next morning was ominous, darkly overcast. Many awoke

with sore lower backs, stiff and in need of a wash. Asao was fine except he didn't like the fact that he was still wearing the same clothes. There really wasn't time to bathe or change since everyone was quickly herded onto flatbed trucks, their doors emblazoned with the words "Neal Evans" in red paint, and taken for a two-hour ride along the switchbacks and roundabouts of the road up Mission Mountain. Mid-morning, one of the prisoners called out that she could make out the Bridge River Valley and Minto. Asao craned his neck to see the lights of a town winking like fireflies at the bottom of a deep valley.

Home for Asao and his mother became a ten-by-ten-foot shack that had been dragged from an abandoned mine a few miles from Minto. Most internees lived in comfortable cabins with indoor plumbing and electricity since they had bought their way into the self-sustaining camp. The Takeharas, however, were there at the charity of their father's former boss, Masato Tokiwa.

★

It had been many years since Tokiwa had first met Gunjiro, but he always remembered how quickly he had taken to the young man. In his Vancouver office, the boss looked closely at the ungainly Gunjiro who stood before him applying for a job in his logging camp up the coast. The adolescent was fresh-faced and right off the boat.

"You been in Canada long?" Tokiwa gruffly asked.

"About a month, bōshin."

"How old are you?"

"Sixteen. But I can do anything you ask," he added quickly.

"Mite young, but you'll soon grow older," Tokiwa said with a smile. "You're on." There was something about the boy the boss liked. Ten years later, Tokiwa made Gunjiro foreman.

★

Probably for old time's sake and at his own expense, Tokiwa had the shack brought to Minto and situated it next to his family cabin with its white picket fence and full garden. Tazuko balked at such generosity. For one thing, she didn't like feeling obligated; for another she felt she was being asked to live in the servants' quarters. She finally accepted when Tokiwa-*san* offered to arrange for her husband's return.

A month later, Gunjiro walked into town, tall and proud, as if he were returning from war, victorious. He had felt disheartened at 100 Mile Camp outside Hope, B.C., slavishly grading the gravel for the Trans-Canada Highway.

"Asao-chan! Ōkiku natta ne?" he roared as he picked up his son. Asao laughed, his cheeks blushing red with the effort. Tazuko looked on with sad moist eyes and hands clasped together. A twinge of pain stabbed her momentarily.

No one ever asked how Tokiwa was able to arrange the reunion, but most thought money had changed hands.

Gunjiro's fortunes seemed to be finally turning. He was with his family far from the government road gang that had taken him from his logging job. In Minto, he managed to join the morning shift at the local sawmill. Money wasn't bad – fifty cents an hour. It would keep food on the table.

Life felt good during the summer of 1942 for Asao. He settled into a comfortable routine of searching for books of any kind and then hiding in the nooks and crannies of the camp to read. Once again, he dreamed of ships braving the vast Seven Seas with their thundering waves.

One night in early October, some of the men were carousing loudly at the Minto Hotel, the *sake* flowing plentifully. The rain outside beat the walls and windows steadily. Minamide, a short fat man with a sparse moustache anchored to a stern, round face, drank to excess, but it was Juntaro, the company driver, who should have practised sobriety that night.

A heavyset man, Juntaro felt he could withstand the effects of much alcohol with ease. It wasn't until his plump face grew bloated, his eyes half closed, that others started to comment.

"Juntaro, you should stop drinking and go to sleep," Minamide suggested. "Tomorrow, we gotta work." He patted his friend's shoulder.

"You sound like my wife," Juntaro slurred. "Who the hell are you to tell me to stop drinking?" He clumsily pushed Minamide's hand away.

"You're drunk and you smell."

Red creases and dark splotches spread across Juntaro's face. He lunged at his antagonist and fell to the floor, unconscious.

The room paused with surprise. Minamide stood and smiled at his friend. "I see you took my advice."

The glare of the morning sun inflicted a penance on the hung-over with a vengeance. Most of the assembled crew had not been invited to the shenanigans of the night before, but Juntaro and Minamide stood swaying in pain.

Juntaro climbed silently into the driver's seat of one of the two covered trucks ready to take everyone to work. The abrupt grind of the ignition caused him to suffer a shooting headache. He rubbed his eyes, palms digging through to the pain. The men in back quickly climbed into their assigned vehicle. They were jovial and looking forward to the day's work. In a few moments, the old Ford and its companion began their usual morning climb of Mission Mountain to A.C. Devine's sawmill.

"You okay, Minamide?" Gunjiro asked with a smile as he smoothed down his greased-back black hair.

"Don't talk to me. The ride's making me sick." His body reeked with the faint perfume of sweat and alcohol.

About half-way up the road, Gunjiro's truck took a sudden turn and teetered for a moment on the edge. Almost in slow motion, it then tipped over the side.

Mud and rock spewed forth as the truck plunged down the mountain slope. The screeching deafened all inside, who really had no idea what was happening. The truck finally rolled and crashed into twin tree trunks lodged among boulders half-way to the bottom. Everything came to a deathly stop.

Gunjiro lay upside down, pinned by equipment, wall braces and torn metal. His arm involuntarily moved and swung about in free space. He felt nothing on the left side of his chest except the weight of debris. After an uncertain length of time, he heard the approach of men rustling down the mountainside, calling as they drew closer.

"Takehara! You all right?"

"I see him. His eyes are open."

With some effort, two of the rescuers loosened Takehara's body from its trap.

Gunjiro cried out. Pain flooded his body. The crew stepped back shocked by the rush of blood staining his shirt.

"Get him up to the truck quick," crew chief Fukunaga ordered. His usually impassive face grimaced with alarm when Minamide's crushed body was next discovered.

"Why can't I see otōsan?" Asao pleaded.

Tazuko turned around. Her face was lined with worry, her brow wet. "He's hurt pretty bad. Maybe later," she promised, even though she knew preparations were under way to transfer him.

Asao cast his eyes downward as he imagined his father covered with blood, his eyes glazed like a dead fish.

Minamide's widow, a frail bat-faced woman of twenty-six, and a few friends prepared the body for cremation. They washed him, clothed him in his best suit and then wrapped him with white linen. They covered his exposed bruises with flour.

Shigeru Noma, camp leader, dressed in a dignified black suit, acted as chairman for the service. His stiffness betrayed no sympathy. A Buddhist minister came in from East Lillooet, the nearest large internment area, to conduct the funeral.

The day was noon-bright; the air crisp. The entire camp of internees gathered on the stony banks of the Bridge River. The water wound its way to the distant Fraser that flowed to the Pacific Ocean. The shoreline trees bristled with the wind. Above the gathering, mountains leaned forward, cutting off the sunlight. Occasionally, gravel slid down the grey expressionless rock faces as if to mourn the freshly dead.

The crowd sighed a collective sorrow for the untimely death of such a young man. Perhaps some held a fear in their hearts of meeting their own fate here in Minto, this blockade to a fulfilled life.

After the minister ended the funeral rites, Noma concluded the service with a note of gratitude. "Though Minamide-san's death seemed senseless and tragic, we can be thankful knowing no one else was lost in the accident."

Hard shoulders and muscled arms pushed open a path through the gathering. Juntaro forced his way to where Minamide's widow stood. Before her, he fell to his knees. "Please, I didn't mean it. It wasn't my fault. Forgive me!" He collapsed under the weight of his guilt, and he lay on the ground, sobbing and whimpering for forgiveness.

The witnesses stood motionless, stunned by Juntaro's behaviour. No one said a word, even after two of the survivors of the crash linked arms around Juntaro's back, pulled him to his feet and led him away. His cries faded into the confines of the surrounding forest.

Noma took advantage of the moment and signalled Fukunaga, who in turn ordered two men to pile wood around the body. The minister began chanting again. Fukunaga poured gasoline over the pyre. His long arm held the torch high before bending down to touch the soaked kindling.

The flames coughed and then spread quickly, lacing into a whole. Soon the fire engulfed the cloth-wrapped body. Asao in front cowered at first. Curiosity made him look again. The ten-year-old boy's eyes widened, his fingers gripped his mother's dress. The heat flushed his skin. He turned his face away and pressed against the flower pattern next to him. He cried silently.

Fukunaga and crew continuously fed the fire with wood. Soon

the crowd disappeared. The shadows of afternoon touched Asao
and two teenaged boys who stayed at a distance to watch the men
work. Asao's eyes remained frozen in horror and wonder. After a
while the two teenagers receded into nearby bushes. Smoke and
black ash drifted above the river in a lazy fashion.

As the pyre smouldered late into the day, the three-man crew
sifted through the ashes for bones. The minister continued to chant
almost in a mechanical fashion.

"*Chikushō*! I hate this work," cursed Fukunaga, the tallest of the
bone diggers. He casually wiped the dirty sweat from his brow
with a handkerchief.

"Yeah, me too," agreed Kego, the fire-plug of the bunch. "Look
I'm drenched." His cotton shirt had darkened with his effort.

"Yare-yare. It's hot work even on a cool day like today," said Minoru Kozai as he sat down on a nearby rock to rest his corpulent
body. "That fire must've been really hot to make such a pile of
ashes."

"Had to make sure Minamide was all burned up. He was a fat
one!"

"He sure liked to eat! I remember he stuffed his face like a pig at
lunchtime," Minoru said without a hint of irony. The trio broke
out laughing.

"Gentlemen! Gentlemen! Have some respect for the dead," the
minister said, his chanting interrupted. Reverend Izumi scolded
them, a stern expression on his usually benign face. "Let's get back
to work."

Fukunaga grimaced as he turned to the distraught *bonsan*,
"Don't worry, sensei, we'll do our job. Minamide was our friend
and … say, who's that boy?"

Everyone turned to the small boy in baggy trousers and white
shirt. Asao snapped out of his spell. His cheeks reddened as he
moved to escape.

"No. No. Come back," they shouted in unison.

Asao stopped in his tracks, his small body shaking slightly. He trained his keen eyes on the approaching men and decided there was no danger. He stepped toward them.

The tall one spoke in a friendly Japanese tone. "I'm Fukunaga. Who are you?"

"Hey, I know him," said Kego. "He's Takehara's kid."

"That so?" asked Fukunaga, his thin face breaking into a smile. Asao bowed his head.

"Sure that's him. Asao's his name. Say, you must be worried about your father."

Reverend Izumi interceded. "All right. I'll take care of the boy. You men finish what you were doing."

The three turned back to the pyre, satisfied with the break from their grim task.

"Asao-chan, what are you doing here? The funeral was over hours ago." The minister's oval face beamed with compassion.

The boy remained silent, but he raised his head, revealing his still red cheeks and damp eyes.

"Ah, I understand," said the minister. His own eyes seemed to smile beneath his bushy eyebrows as he led the boy to a nearby shaded area. "You *are* worried about your father."

★

Gunjiro lay in his bed motionless. His damaged body seemed to slump into the mattress. He eyed each passerby with suspicion. They seemed to speak a very difficult English. He caught the meaning of only a few phrases.

Since coming to Canada as a young man of sixteen, he had spent most of his time amongst the Japanese in Little Tokyo and in the lumber camps. At one point he had tried to learn English, thinking it would be easy. He prided himself on learning quickly. One of his friends had told him about lessons at the Language School on Alexander Street. However, when he found he was not a quick study, he soon grew tired of the incomprehensible English words and the tiresome posturing of the teachers. He was a man after all.

In any case, communicating in English was not a concern in the hospital. He didn't have the breath to form words. Bandages were wrapped tightly around his chest, making movement minimal at best. The accident had crushed the left side of his rib-cage. He was lucky to be alive.

The road to Kamloops had been long, dusty and uneven. Every bump of the truck had caused spikes of pain to drive through his chest. Gunjiro's strength withered with every swerve and turn. Tears filled his bright, intense eyes, blurring them, blinding them. His attendants, two co-workers and Minto's simple-minded constable, Fred Johnson, could barely endure his screams during the hundred-plus miles to Kamloops.

After some explanation by the red-haired RCMP constable, the hospital doctors admitted Gunjiro and attended to his needs.

The patient had no visitors. Nurses and interns generally ignored him, attending him only to feed him and to prevent bed sores. The whitewashed, silent room that smelled of talcum powder and alcohol closed in on his consciousness.

> *Bastard ketō! What're you lookin' at? You want to kill me. I know. But I'll show you. I'll go home again. I'll go home. The pain. If only the pain would go away!*

Gunjiro's only pleasure was to gaze at the night sky through a nearby window. When the moon first appeared full, his mind drifted to his father. "Funny," he whispered to himself, "I haven't thought of him since I left Japan."

Otōsan towered over his three children, especially Gunjiro, the youngest. His long white beard and narrow-set eyes made him look like a demon. Gunjiro was afraid of him. Still, he remembered the simple rice farmer had from time to time composed poetry. *Waka*, he called them. Poems he wrote and recited during times of joy, distress and sorrow. Gunjiro faced the moon and honoured his father's memory.

> *Sleep. Night with your great gift, take the pain away. Let me sleep so that when I wake I'll see my wife's face, my little son's face. Dear wife, I'm broken into pieces and taken away from you, but at least we see the same full moon.*

★

With one of his large hands, Reverend Izumi gently took hold of Asao's two small ones. He glowed with understanding. "Don't worry, Asao-chan, your father will be fine. The doctors in Kamloops will take good care of him."

Asao felt tears tracing the curve of his nose. He bowed and let the rivulets fall to the ground. He imagined the wood and body curling as if squirming away from the flames. The black ash turning to grey and crumbling into dust. He shook involuntarily.

"Sensei?" he asked weakly. "What happens to Minamide-san now?"

"Well, we'll scatter his remains over the river and he'll float away to the ocean."

"He'll float on the ocean forever?"

"Yes, I suppose he will. Asleep and without pain."

"Oh how brave …"

"Asao-chan, where have you been?" Tazuko asked while slicing green onions at the eating table.

He said nothing. He just stood in the doorway staring at his mother.

Tazuko groaned as she stood up. She warmed her bulging upper stomach with a free hand. "Don't just stand there, go wash up. Dinner will be soon."

Asao plodded outside to the pump. He filled a shallow metal pan and scooped up a pool of cool, clear water. He held his breath as he

splashed his face. The water tingled his supple skin as he repeated
the process a few times before reaching for the towel hanging on a
nearby nail.

He jerked to attention when he heard a sudden crash come from
inside the house. He dropped the coarse terry cloth towel as he
stepped through the door. A low moan vibrated along the
floor-boards. He tried to scream but nothing came out. He stood
mute, frozen into paralysis. His mother lay before him covered
with dinner preparations and writhing in pain.

With difficulty, she twisted around to her son. "Asao-chan, go
get Tokiwa-no obāsan. Next door," Tazuko gasped, as she struggled to stand. Her arms crumpled; she slumped to the floor, her
face contorted with agony.

Asao backed out of the shack, his legs shrinking with numbness
at every step. He turned and stood just outside. His words choked
but they were not needed. A matronly woman with a few bags of
groceries came to the door. Mrs. Tokiwa, white hair pulled tightly
into a bun, had happened to be passing by when she heard the
commotion.

"Takehara-san, what's wrong?" she asked with concern.

"Sharp pain. My gallstones ..." Tazuko managed to say.

"*Ah ra.* I'll get Noma-san."

Two days later, Dr. Miyazaki came to Minto from East Lillooet.
Tazuko's face was damp with sweat, her body emaciated from constant vomiting. The good doctor adjusted his round wire glasses,
pushed back the thin hair emphasizing his receding hairline, and
spoke quietly to his patient. Mrs. Tokiwa stood nearby with Asao.

"I'm afraid you need an operation. The gallstones must be pretty
bad to cause you so much pain."

"How can I have an operation here?" she asked, her lips trembling.

"Not here. In Vancouver. I'll arrange things with the authorities ..."

"No. Not Vancouver. My son. I can't leave Asao ..."

"Don't worry," assured Mrs. Tokiwa. "I'll take care of him."

"Take me to Kamloops, where my husband is," she pleaded with the doctor.

"The hospital in Vancouver has the proper facilities," he smiled. "Don't worry, everything'll be all right."

Asao's eyes began to well up with tears. He tried to go to his mother but couldn't. A knot formed in his stomach.

★

Tazuko was barely conscious lying on a metal gurney in a dark institutional green hallway of St. Mary's Hospital, Vancouver. She was dimly aware of grey figures moving past. Gibberish rained on her ears.

A collage of images entered her mind. Most were of her son Asao, a small rose-cheeked boy with smudged knees and shy features. Her eyes squeezed tight, her small hands clenched involuntarily. Fishing nets draped across the dreamscape. She came from a small village called Mihama on the Sea of Japan coast. Her father, a successful fisherman with a small fleet of boats, had called her to him one day during her adolescence. The *tatami* was golden in his room. He sat in the middle, his short legs tucked underneath his long torso.

"Tazuko-chan," he said as he rubbed his balding head. "It is time for you to marry. I have nothing to give you except a suitable husband."

"Yes, otōsan," she answered, having anticipated the moment.

"I've made arrangements with the Takehara family. You will marry their third son, Gunjiro."

There was nothing to say. It was her duty to obey her father. She bowed and left the room. She kept her concerns to herself even though Gunjiro's prospects disturbed her to no end. It was one thing to marry a poor third son, but to marry a poor man from a foreign country ... Intolerable! Canada was a land of brutal white devils and coarse Japanese men.

"Okāsan, how could you let this happen to me?" she finally blurted out.

"Now Tazuko-chan. You mustn't complain," her mother said compassionately. "You are not of this family any more. Your husband is young and strong. You'll be rich in Canada."

There was no choice. Her eyes dried immediately. She glared at her mother and left the house. She bolted across the grounds as fast as she could. At a safe distance, she stretched her arms up straight, her fists clenched and shaking. She vowed never to return, never to express sorrow again.

★

After Tazuko had agreed to the operation, Constable Johnson had wired his superior in Lillooet, a Sergeant Ferguson, to request immediate permission to escort Dr. Miyazaki and his patient to Vancouver. The usually slow moving Mountie was up to his neck in police work. In fact, he was investigating, at that moment, a mysterious fire that had burned down Etsuji Morii's house. But as soon as he saw Tazuko's condition, he acted quickly. Morii had probably deserved it anyway, he reasoned.

Permission came right away. It took two days for Johnson and the doctor to transport the patient to the coast. Tazuko, numbed by pain killers, didn't realise she was retracing the route she had taken when she was first exiled.

Dr. Miyazaki had spent his internship at St. Mary's Hospital, an imposing gothic building in east-end Vancouver. No one in Admitting remembered him; fortunately, the head nurse did. His patient in good hands (or so he thought), Dr. Miyazaki left the city with Constable Johnson as soon as he could.

"What is this person doing here?" asked the Mother Superior of a passing nurse. During her daily rounds, Mother Catherine, a stout woman with clear eyes and wide mouth, had come across a patient with irregular breathing, matted hair, and a cold pallor. The tiny Japanese woman was nearly unconscious.

"Don't know," replied the lean young nurse, disinterested behind steel-rimmed glasses.

"How long has she been here?" Mother Catherine snapped. She

quickly inspected the chart hanging from the gurney. "Oh my Lord, she's been lying here for six hours! She needs immediate attention."

"Well Sister, I'm not touching her." The nurse turned away.

"Wait a minute!" Mother Catherine called. "What's the matter with you. There's a patient dying here."

"A *Jap* patient," cried the nurse. "I'm not aiding the enemy."

Mother Catherine cursed under her breath and ran to the intercom. Within minutes, two nuns in black robes responded. The three then wheeled Tazuko toward an operating room.

★

Asao sat alone in the cabin on his favourite chair, a short-legged wooden one salvaged from the Vancouver boarding house. He rubbed the wood mindlessly, only half aware of the scratches and gouges.

His mother's pain frightened him but it wasn't new. In Vancouver, she had suffered from the "stomach rocks" twice before. At that time, he had stayed with family friends down the hall.

Perhaps it was the darkness of the mountains, the distance from cities, or the knowledge that both of his parents were hurt – Asao just couldn't shake the tears. His family life had been filled with separation, but this time he felt the void of abandonment.

The incandescent light of the evening sky threw the surrounding mountains into darkness. Minto's lights flickered on as night pulled its curtain across the valley.

Asao lay in bed after a simple meal of *miso shiru*, fish and rice prepared by a harried Tokiwa-*no obāsan*. At dinner, Masato Tokiwa, a grumpy man with grey stubble and a slight paunch, had presided over the meal in undershirt, slippers and wool pants with suspenders. Mrs. Tokiwa fussed over the food, manoeuvring carefully around the cramped kitchen, adjusting her tightly pinned-up hair at the same time. It was difficult to enjoy the meal. Asao had no appetite. The Tokiwas were nice enough people, but they scared him. Tokiwa-*san* never talked to him, he growled. He would never allow Tokiwa-*no obāsan* to hug him like *okāsan*. Asao pulled the covers tighter around his chin.

The bed was soft, held in place by a corner of the room. He curled his body into a ball as he thought of the funeral pyre, his father, his mother. His stomach was a deep well of emptiness. He stared into the murk of the room seeing images in the shadows. His hands gripped handfuls of bedding. His face began to sweat. A light burned in the hallway outside his room. Muttering voices were carried to the dim regions of the cabin on the soft movement of air.

> *What do we do about the boy? He's not our responsibility. His parents are in a bad way ... probably both will die ... what then ... we're not relatives ... send him to Japan ... yes, that's it ... his relatives will have to take him in ... to Japan ... parents are probably dead ... he's an orphan ...*

Wolves howled outside. The walls moved closer to the boy. He hiccuped and sobbed, jerking the patchwork comforter intermittently.

> *Okāsan. Otōsan. Dead. Burn them up in the fire. Toss them into the ocean. Cold, deep water. Across the ocean to Japan. Burn me up. White-caps lapping at my bones. I'm not that brave.*

Wood crackled in the fire. The smell of burning cedar hung suspended above the comforter and sheets. He felt his skin sizzle.

Asao threw off the covers of his bed in a panic. His entire body tingled. He sat up slapping his arms to extinguish the sensation. The sweat from his forehead blurred his vision.

In the shadows, a figure loomed out of the night, floating before him, spreading in all directions like an ink-emitting octopus. The impenetrable black threatened to envelop the entire room. Asao rubbed his eyes and fought the urge to scream. Smoke poured into the emptiness. The boy coughed, gulping for air. A moment later, a soft voice spoke to him.

Asao, the ocean is warm. Join me in my sleep.

The cold air gripped him. He shivered. His face feverish, he pushed himself into the corner. Minamide-san? Could it be? Minamide-san? The shadow dissipated, but the smoke streamed into his nostrils. He choked again. The voice grew more insistent.

Join me. There's no pain. Your parents are here. Come.

His stomach tightened. He bolted from the bed and ran through the hallway out into the waiting bosom of night.

★

Gunjiro and Tazuko recovered and returned to Minto about the same time. They learned of their son's disappearance from Mrs. Tokiwa. Gunjiro, his hair now grey, had aged visibly, yet he remained stoic.

"*Ganbari-nasai!*" he encouraged his wife. "We can have another child."

Tazuko was frantic and ran. She stopped before the mountains and called his name. "Asao-chan! Asao-chan!" Her echo was her only answer. She cried for days on end, until eventually she accepted the silence.

Constable Johnson had made inquiries. It seemed no one saw or heard the boy leave camp, not even the Tokiwas, who could not comprehend how Asao had left the cabin without their knowledge. Search parties were formed but nothing was found. The only clue to the mystery was the lingering haze of smoke in Asao's room.

Kangaroo Court

Tomiko's hair is a streak of night curving along the landscape of her back. When the wind kicks up, night turns into black fire. Her eyes are half-moons saddened by compassion. Her laugh is the sound of gentle rain on a bamboo roof. Her bare legs strain sinuously when induced to run. Her slender arms tighten around her flat abdomen to sculpt her breasts into small mounds on a rolling landscape. Her complexion shimmers pale against the colours of day.

Men would do anything for a woman like Tomiko.

★

Tetsuo Kozai was born in Vancouver twenty-three years before World War II began. A son of Powell Street grocers, he learned the ins and outs of the business quickly and adopted the name "Bill" in an effort to become "Canadian." One month after Pearl Harbor, he realised the deceptive nature of his vanity.

The B.C. Security Commission authorities categorised him separately from his family because he lived on his own. He was then forced to carry his allotted bags of personal possessions inland, 350 miles away from his family, to suffer the winter of '42 alone.

"I'm a Canadian, God damn it!" he shouted. "Someone's gonna pay for this!" The wind howled, choking his angry cries. Snow swirled around his legs as he quickly shoved his bags into a military tent. The canvas fluttered with complaint, and skeleton frames in a field beside Lemon Creek creaked against the raging blizzard.

Two men huddled in a corner as they evaluated their new tent-mate. "We're Japs to them or haven't you heard there's a war on?" said the small lump who popped his head out of his wool jacket like a turtle.

"Yeah, I heard there's a war on," Tetsuo snapped. "God, it's cold. Those bastards that did this to us!"

"Close the flap!" complained the other lump buried beneath blankets.

The turtle rolled to his knees. "Yeah, they're bastards, but what can we do? *Shikataganai ne?*"

"You *are* a Jap if you think like that."

"You'll learn."

"What?"

The small man offered his hand. "I'm Buck Komiyama. My *otōsan's* the minister here." He was friendly. His thin angular face was all smiles and moustache. "The frozen guy in the corner is Mutt."

"Glad to meet ya, Mutt. I'm Bill from Vancouver."

The lump under the blankets mumbled a greeting. He preferred keeping warm to exposing his identity to the cold.

"How long you fellahs been here?"

"We were part of the first party to get here," Buck explained. "We put up the tents and we're putting together the cabins."

"How about them cabins? When do we get in?"

"Keep your shirt on. With this snow, in about a month – with your help!"

"Don't worry, I'll keep more than my shirt on," replied Tetsuo.

In the months that followed Tetsuo's arrival, the record cold winter of 1942 smashed against the rows of jerry-built wooden shacks that comprised the Lemon Creek internment camp about seven miles outside Slocan, British Columbia. Green, freshly cut wood shrivelled and cracked in the tempest wind. Pernicious drafts scrabbled through the gaping holes like wolves hungry for warm bodies in thin clothing.

Tetsuo thought it ironic that Mutt Shimoda contracted pneumonia. Buck laughed when he guessed Mutt caught it trying to keep warm by shivering in bed, refusing to work. He recovered when warmer weather brought lighter tasks and more inmates to the camp.

Each flat-roofed shack had a door and window, a tin stove, wood-frame bunkbeds with wet straw mattresses, and not much else. Internees spent much of that winter becoming accustomed to living with one or two other families in the same box, learning to trim and light kerosene lamps, breaking through the ice and hauling water from nearby Lemon Creek.

About late March, a break in the weather allowed the prisoners a chance to brighten their lives. A dance was announced, to be held in the newly constructed schoolhouse, a tall one-room building in the middle of the camp.

The men covered the crude tables with white paper. A couple of the older women supervised the young in decorating the walls with Christmas ornaments and crepe paper which the internees had included amongst their hastily packed possessions. Records too. It was amazing how many people had brought 78s to Lemon Creek, even though all electronic devices, such as record players, were forbidden. Useless, but they wanted pieces of home with them.

Jack Duggan, the RCMP constable, provided the player. The music swelled and subsided throughout the night. "Take the A Train" drew guys and gals out onto the dance floor. The moon rose high above snow-drifts and expanses of ice. Mountains held up a clear, star-filled sky. Nearby trees shook loose their snow to the beat of the luxurious swing music.

Tetsuo Bill Kozai, the son of Little Tokyo grocers, was tall for a Japanese, five feet ten inches, and possessed a muscular upper torso from lifting heavy boxes and constructing the camp. He kept his hair short, a neat brush-cut. His face was thin with a long nose and small tight mouth. He wore wire glasses, the result of reading small-print pulp novels by candlelight. Some thought him handsome.

One thing for sure, he wasn't shy. He slid across the floor and stood before a pretty girl with long hair curled at the ends. "Hi. I'm Bill. You wanna dance?"

She looked at him with her long-lashed eyes and nodded consent. The couple drifted easily into the crowd as the Modernaires crooned a slow version of "Don't Get Around Much Anymore."

"Say, you are a pretty one. What's your name?" Bill asked as he pulled her in close.

"Tommy."

"Tommy? That's a funny name for a girl."

"A nickname. Tomiko Watanabe is my real name."

"Oh. Where you from?"

"Haney. My parents are ... were farmers back there."

The hint of a country drawl became obvious to him. "Are they here?"

"*Otōsan* is at Three Valley Gap. My *okāsan* is over there watching us," she said as she motioned to a corner with her head.

Bill glanced around quickly. He stepped back a pace and held her at arm's length. Tomiko laughed.

"Say, you wanna get some punch?" Bill asked, a little embarrassed. He felt the watchful eyes of a parent.

"Sure."

"Maybe you can introduce me to your mom."

"Maybe."

As the couple made their way to the confections table, Bill nodded to Mrs. Watanabe. Tomiko smiled. Mrs. Watanabe smiled back. People remarked how good the couple looked together. At the table, Tomiko's fresh face caught the candlelight and her beauty shimmered. It also gleamed in the eyes of a dark, brooding figure surveying the crowd from the doorway.

By the time spring arrived with its warm light, Lemon Creek had expanded to include outhouses perfumed with the pungent odour of lime, a Buddhist temple, a United Church, and a grocery store with a crude veranda to display fresh vegetables. The rolling hills that acted as a boundary to the campsite turned green in the sun and the surrounding forests that ran to the horizon buzzed with new life.

With spring came also opportunity. Bill Kozai's Vancouver experience made him the ideal candidate for the job of grocery store clerk, but first he had to be hired by the village leader, the *sonchō*.

"Where you from, boy?" Isamu Sasaki growled. The office in the back of the grocery store was small and cluttered with the papers and furniture of business.

"Vancouver, sir," Bill said nervously.

"Kozai? I think I know your family. You the poor ones with the drunk for a father?"

The insult was clear, but Bill knew better than to complain. "No sir, you're thinking of the Koyata family. They live near us."

Sasaki sat back before letting out a laugh. "I don't know any Koyata family or your family for that matter! Here's what, you can work for me in this store. You can live in the room next to this office. Keep your mouth shut, keep the shelves full, the prices right and the place clean, and I'll be happy. I'll collect the receipts once a week."

Bill accepted readily.

★

Many of the stores in Vancouver's Little Tokyo had given credit to their customers who couldn't pay until the harvests of fish, logs or crops were in. Long lists of debtors were used by the shopkeepers to secure loans to buy supplies. The banks saw the lists as good collateral since the Japanese Canadians were hard working and honest. They paid their debts. When the war began, the Mounties padlocked every door and confiscated all inventory. At the same time, the B.C. Security Commission moved to impound fishing boats and to restrict movement. No one could do business any longer. Debts could not be paid. The banks foreclosed.

Isamu Sasaki seized the moment. He knew the Commission didn't know what to do with the Japanese foodstuffs and so moved to buy them on the cheap, using his RCMP contacts – students in his *judō* club. Eventually, he transported everything to the internment camps, inflated the prices and made a fortune.

Food profiteering gave him status and a fearful respect. The Lemon Creek internees felt compelled to make him *sonchō*, village leader.

★

In his job, Bill found the work tedious, made so by the constant re-pricing of the items. Everything seemed to grow more expensive every day. But he learned to accept his circumstances. Most of the little money he made went to his parents in Tashme internment camp, 350 miles away.

He spent his days maintaining inventory, sweeping out the building, helping customers, and thinking about his girl. He was happiest when he had the time to be with her.

"It's very nice here," Tomiko said as she brushed her hair aside. A ticklish wind played with it.

"Nice? What's so nice about it?" Bill scowled as he picked at the grass atop Anderson Hill. "I feel like I'm in prison."

"Don't be such a Gloomy Gus! Winter is gone and the warm sun is back! How can you complain?" Tomiko sat with a straight back, her flower print dress settled about her ankle socks and flats. She kept her arms in close to hide the frayed cuffs.

"Yeah, that sure was a bad winter," Bill agreed. "You weren't here at the very beginning, but seemed like every morning, I'd wake up freezing in my tent."

"Look, Bill," she said, "there's crocuses growing near the edge of camp." Her delight flushed her face.

"Yeah, nice."

"Oh Bill, look at those mountains," she gestured. "The horizon. That's our future."

"What?" he asked, seeing only her clear eyes.

"This won't last forever," she proclaimed, pointing at the camp. "One day we'll be free to really make it on our own. We've got to look to what's beyond those mountains!" she said with conviction. "Oh don't you see, being here is the best thing for us Japanese? We don't need Little Tokyo! It was a ghetto."

"Little Tokyo? A ghetto? What do you know about anything?" he responded abruptly. "You're from that hick town Haney where people live to gossip about each other."

Tomiko glared at him. She bristled with anger. "William Kozai, I've been to Vancouver ... to Powell Street many times. I've seen the broken-down houses, the drinking halls and ... and who knows what else!"

"Tommy ..."

"We were in that awful place, Hastings Park!" She cupped her face in her hands.

Bill moved to comfort her. "Aw Tommy, I didn't mean anything by what I said."

She continued to sob as the recent past surfaced in her thoughts.

> *Tomiko sat on her mean cot in her assigned stall in the cavernous livestock building. She hadn't bathed since confined the week before. No plumbing for showers or baths. Surrounding her, beyond the makeshift blanket walls, were wailing babies with distraught mothers suffering from nervous exhaustion. Everywhere hung the fetid stench of long-gone animals. She stared with hollow eyes, her hair tangled and dull, waiting for her mother who had gone, as she had done every passing day, to find out when they were to entrain for parts unknown. Any place would be better, they imagined.*

"Tommy," he said finally. "I'm sorry. I know the Pool was awful. It's just that I'm such a sad apple. Here I am running a crummy shack of a grocery store which I don't even own. I've got no future. How can I ever ask you ..."

"Shhhh," Tomiko implored. She tenderly clasped his hand. They embraced. He drew in her sweet breath and the aroma of her skin, scented with a mild soap. Their lips met with light kisses that rapidly grew more urgent. He became conscious of her smooth arms as he moved to squeeze her breast; she resisted and then relaxed. Breathing quickened. He dropped his hand to her dress, tracing her knee before slipping beneath to the beginning of thigh. She shuddered "No".

Bill shook his head, regained his composure and clasped his hands together in a tight grip.

From a distance, eyes observed.

★

Isamu Sasaki was not considered a handsome man. His face, badly scarred from a logging accident, had earlier provoked catcalls from children and unkind comments from adults. Eventually, his *judō* ability intimidated all into silence.

His fire-plug body was solid muscle. His face, apart from the scar down the left side, was remarkably fierce despite close-set eyes, a weak chin and flat nose. His hair was cropped short as was the style around the *judō dōjō*.

His ambition had always been to be feared if not respected. To this end, he bullied his way around Little Tokyo in Vancouver with the help of several of his students from the *judō* club. His talent for leadership inspired many to join him, and the money from various schemes kept them loyal. Still, there were a few who opposed him.

"You Ted Shiraishi?" Sasaki barked as he confronted the tall young Asahi baseball player in front of Benny's Cafe.

"Yeah. What of it?" Ted answered, his keen eyes squinting a challenge.

"I want you to stop complaining in that damn newspaper *The New Canadian* about my judō club."

"You guys are a bunch of thugs!" Ted said, while nervously smoothing his hair. "You should be run out of town."

"Sō ka?" Sasaki reared back to deliver a blow.

Ted avoided the punch and burst down Powell Street in a desperate run. Sasaki, joined by two of his boys, caught up to the athlete six blocks away. In a blind alley, the three ganged up on the young man.

Ted blocked the first hits, but was soon overwhelmed by the barrage of blows from all sides. He fell to the ground, numbed by kicks to the stomach and groin.

"That'll teach all the bastards against me," Sasaki hissed over the slumped body.

★

Sasaki felt he could do and have anything he wanted, and what he wanted now was a woman only another kind of man could ever hope to win. "Watanabe-san," he greeted as he bowed, "atsui ne?" His Japanese seemed perfunctory, merely small talk, even as he wiped the heat from his brow. "This summer's too damned hot!" The *sonchō* rubbed his feet on the bare floor before awkwardly moving farther into the spare but neat shack at the edge of the camp. Sumiko Watanabe and her daughter had managed to bring only clothes, pots and pans and a few precious items from their farm in Haney.

"Welcome. Please sit down," offered the middle-aged woman. Sumiko wore her hair in a tight knot atop her head. Her face was smooth, with a high nose bridge straddled by wire-rimmed glasses. "May I serve you some ocha?"

"Sure."

Sumiko boiled the water and selected a suitable green tea. On a tray, she placed a tin pot, blue Japanese cups and some rice crackers and digestives. She gingerly presented the arrangement on the eating table before the *sonchō*.

"There's not much here, but please help yourself," she said as she poured the tea.

"These are wonderful cups!" Sasaki remarked, admiring the deep blue colour and patterns of gold.

"My mother's. They're about the only Japanese things I managed to bring."

"Watanabe-san, I'll tell you why I'm here," he began. "I notice you have a daughter. I saw her at the dance last March." He chose a cup and drank quickly. Once empty, he fondled it in his hand, as he paused to choose his words. "Your daughter needs settling. She must be a worry. She's a bit," he hesitated, "wild, wouldn't you say?"

Sumiko was unmoved.

"I've seen her with ... well, the wrong kind. A bad future for her if she acts hastily."

Sumiko eyed the floor.

"Listen, I'm of a marrying age. Perhaps you will agree to allow me to marry her?"

Sumiko coughed slightly. His smile was too much to bear. Her small hands clasped together in her lap. "She is a bit young, eighteen."

Sasaki jerked his back straight. "Are you saying I'm too old for her? I may be thirty-two but I have money, lots of money, and I'm strong, strong like a bull!"

Alarmed, she was quick to respond. "No, sonchō, it's not like that. I'm afraid her youth may not agree to such a union at this time."

"Well, I'm sure you'll find a way to convince her!" Sasaki stood up and swaggered to the door. "It's agreed then. I will marry Tomiko."

Sumiko bowed. Sasaki bowed curtly and pocketed the blue cup as he left. Sumiko remained silent.

"*Okāsan*! How could you ask me to marry that horrible little man!"

"Tomiko, now you have more respect. He is sonchō here," Sumiko said in a mildly chastising Japanese. Her face frowned as she reached to help her daughter comb her hair.

"But he's so old!"

"Not so old."

"And ugly ..." She shuddered slightly.

"Your father is seven years older than me."

"Sasaki is older than that."

"Sasaki has money and will be able to provide for you after the war. What choice do you have?"

"I'll provide for me after the war!" she declared, her eyes defiant. "Besides, I love Bill!"

"The grocery store clerk? *Ahō*! He has no future." Sumiko laid down the comb and moved away. "Love won't put food on the table."

"Love will help us face the future," she declared self-consciously.

"Ahhh," Sumiko scoffed and left the shack to tend to the washing. In her heart, she could understand her daughter's objections, but given the present situation, she knew marriage to Sasaki was for the best. She shuddered when she thought how the *sonchō* was going to react.

Sasaki slammed his fist hard on his desk when word reached him of Tomiko's refusal. His underlings were startled by his ferocity.

"It's that bastard clerk I hired for the grocery store," he hissed. "I've seen them together." He paused ominously. "She doesn't appreciate what I can provide her. There's no future with ... with ... what's his name?"

"Kozai," supplied a voice from the early evening dark.

"That's right. I'm going to have to deal with this mushi."

"Why, *bōshin*? Why do you want to bother with him?"

A hand unhinged and lashed out hard. The insolent inferior fell to the floor with a thud.

"Because I want his girlfriend, you idiot! I need a wife and I don't want an ugly one, understand?"

The underling receded. Several other figures moved about the small cabin. Some shifted on couches provided by the Commission. Others shuffled across the floor to stand by the open window.

"*Yoshi!*" Sasaki abruptly concluded. "Bring Kozai to the schoolhouse around eleven o'clock tonight. I want all of you there too!"

"Bōshin, what're you gonna do to him?"

"You're gonna be the jury, and I'm putting him on trial."

"For what?"

"Who cares? I'll think of something."

An excited murmur began.

"Now shut up. No outsiders, hear me!" Sasaki turned his attention to his assistant. "Nakamura, I've got a special job for you." He chuckled as the darkness folded in on the conspiracy.

The crescent moon rose high that night. Tomiko tossed as she drifted beneath the surface of sleep. A face broadened in front of her. Its breathing quickened, a hot exhaust. Rough hands moved beneath the sheets and pulled at her chemise. Her legs

*shifted away but the hands were insistent. She screamed but
heard no noise. Her arms pulled against some restraint. Her legs
were parted. On her face, she felt the jagged edges of a scar. She
woke with a start, her face blurred with cold sweat.*

The faint light of the sickle moon allowed shadowy figures to
creep through the compound without detection. Bill, enjoying his
privacy, was reading a well-thumbed copy of a Buck Rogers adventure in his room at the back of the grocery store. A rough
knock interrupted the flow of words. He was more annoyed than
apprehensive as he moved to answer the call. As soon as he creaked
the door open, hands reached in and grabbed him by the front of
his shirt. They dragged him along the floor and through the door
to the outside. He fought in vain against the sour-smelling presence that pulled him along. Sasaki's gang. He started to cry out but
hands stifled all sound.

Before he knew it, he was sitting in a chair in the middle of the
schoolhouse. He could just make out the men standing in the surrounding darkness, a single dull light bulb just above him limiting
his vision. Not daring to move, he shook involuntarily, his skin
crackling with uneasiness.

A black figure swelled in front of him, his shadow dominating
the room. Everyone became quiet.

"Kozai, Tetsuo," boomed a familiar voice.

"Sasaki-san?"

"Shut up!" Sasaki commanded in staccato Japanese. "You are to
listen. You'll have a chance to defend yourself later."

Defend myself? he thought. What have I done? What's going on
here? What am I doing here?

Sasaki came forward and turned his back on Bill. "Gentlemen of
Lemon Creek, sitting before you is the most disgusting insect you
will ever come across. He is shit. He is worse than shit. He is the
insect that digs in shit!"

Grumbles came from the small crowd. The accused began to
shake again and twist his head around even though he couldn't discern anyone's identity.

"He steals from all of us in camp here. He price-gouges. One dollar for a small bottle of shoyu! Three dollars for five pounds of rice! He raises the prices on the quiet and pockets the profits."

"No," Bill protested. "You're the one who ..."

A hand slapped his mouth into silence.

"Give me a guilty verdict so that I can deal with this *kusotare!*"

The faceless ones erupted with a roar of approval.

"Thank you, gentlemen. Well Kozai, what do you have to say for yourself? Are you ready to admit your guilt?"

Bill squirmed in his seat. He dried his sweating hands on his thighs. He looked to the pale moonlight seeping through the solitary window and imagined it to be the last sight of the outside he would see. He shook in premonition of what was about to happen. "Sonchō, what do you want of me? I didn't do anything!"

Another slap of the hand silenced him. "See, the coward practically admits his guilt!"

"Please," Bill begged, almost crying. A quick blow to the mouth. He tasted blood.

"Are you ready to admit to your crime?"

Shikataganai. Bill realised he had only one option and broke into a sudden plea as he fell to his knees, "Sonchō, please forgive me! Please forgive me!" He began to bow repeatedly, asking for forgiveness.

"Such a coward," Sasaki spat. "Since you admit your guilt, everyone will know your shame. From this day forward, you will be known as *Tako*, the creature with eight arms that steals the food from everyone's mouth." He began to laugh. The entire room rumbled with laughter. "That is your punishment."

Bill felt the rush of blood to his face. He lowered his head and slumped over. Hands again pulled him to his feet and pushed him to the door. As he was thrown into the coolness outside, derisive laughter echoed in the hollow mountain air.

Two steps later and a crushing blow across his chest dropped him to the ground. A second cracked the bone of his upper arm. A third broke over his knee. Shadows swung wooden clubs, two-by-fours, and made contact at will. He recoiled in pain until he fell into blessed unconsciousness. The unseen thugs withdrew from his stillness.

★

Reverend Masami Komiyama and his son Buck, having heard the commotion, left their cabin to investigate. They found Bill in a heap on the ground.

"*Otōsan*, it's Kozai-*san*!" Buck exclaimed as he knelt beside the body. "He's hurt real bad."

The minister's strong, husky appearance belied his gentle touch. He bent over and manipulated Bill so that he was lying flat on his back. Blood stained the clothes; the bones grotesquely positioned. "Pretty bad," he muttered in English. "Go get Duggan-*san*."

The sleepy Mountie stumbled in the dark as he approached the scene. The sight of the broken boy woke him up abruptly. "Don't worry," he assured the minister, "I'll get him to Kamloops. There's a good hospital there."

The trio carefully lifted Bill and carried him to the Mountie's car. He moaned as he was folded into the back seat of the old Ford. The motor turned over quickly and soon the vehicle crept through the darkness; night collapsed in its wake.

Constable Duggan investigated immediately but found only silence. After learning Bill was unable to speak, the constable cajoled people to talk by telling them of his condition: all four limbs broken, several ribs fractured, nearly blind in one eye and multiple lacerations about the body. The doctors felt his recovery would take at least a year. But to no avail. No one in camp had any knowledge of the incident.

He gave up after a week. Even though Duggan himself suspected what had happened, evidence or testimony was needed to take action.

Sasaki flew into a rage when confronted by Sumiko Watanabe. "What do you mean your daughter won't see me?" He hurled his blue cup against the wall, smashing it to pieces.

Sumiko cowered and bowed timidly. "I'm sorry, but you must understand, she won't marry you," she said respectfully, mindful of her heirloom's fate.

"Why not?" he bellowed louder.

"Because you ..." Her voice faltered.

"Well?"

"Because of what happened to Kozai-san."

"What!" he growled. "What's that got to do with me?"

"Everyone knows." She turned away, expecting the worst. Her lips trembled.

"*Shimatta ne!*" Sasaki cursed. He squeezed his fists. "Get the hell out of my sight. I tell you what, I won't have your daughter. She has a busaikuna face. Get out! Get out!"

Sasaki roared. Sumiko cowered and left quietly. Sasaki's men withdrew unnoticed.

"People of Lemon Creek," began Buck Komiyama, the minister's son, "a terrible thing has happened to an innocent young man."

A murmur of agreement rippled through the standing-room-only crowd in the sparsely furnished shack that served as the Buddhist Church.

"Bill Kozai was nearly beaten to death for no good reason. Are we going to stand for this? Are we going to let Sasaki get away with this?"

"Why now? He's been price-gouging us since the beginning and we did nothing!" an unidentified voice rang out.

"Enough is enough," Buck responded.

The crowd roared.

"He's right!" a young man agreed. "We can't let this kind of man take our money and then do anything he wants to any one of us! He can't get away with this!"

"Let's give him a taste of his own medicine. His men won't help him now!"

"Yeah. Beat him! Beat him to the ground!" Voices collected into one sentiment.

"No!" pleaded an unlikely voice. Tomiko stood before the dais, wringing her hands. "Buck, your father wouldn't act this way!" She turned and addressed the mob. "I don't like Sasaki any more than you, but please, you won't be any better than him if you do this!" The calls of "Beat him! Beat him!" continued. Tomiko withdrew.

Reverend Komiyama moved from his position in the church doorway to stand beside his son. He clapped his hands together, the sharp rap silencing the din.

The good minister considered a second before speaking. "The girl's right. We must not take the law into our own hands. Let's call on the authorities to deal with him. Constable Duggan is a decent sort."

"No!" complained an unseen man. "Sasaki's gouged us nearly to death. I've lost most of my savings."

The crowd grumbled.

"We've all been victimised by this man. Are we to become his victimiser now?" reasoned the minister. "Look where we are. In prison. We have accepted our fate all too easily. Now we have a chance to use that fate to get ourselves some justice. Let Constable Duggan deal with this. Answer his questions. We will at least be able to sleep at night."

The crowd groaned in reluctant agreement and began to mutter amongst themselves. Reverend Komiyama put his arm around his son's shoulders and smiled. "Now, they are talking. Everything will be all right."

★

The sun burned brightly at its peak. The air was heavy, hot. The wind soothed as two Mounties escorted the handcuffed Sasaki to a waiting truck. The internees had listened to reason, and once they saw that Sasaki was truly alone, his men unwilling to do his petty bidding anymore, they testified freely to Constable Duggan. No trial was necessary. Duggan requested a transfer for a troublemaker, a Japanese National, and that was that. Sasaki's destination was a concentration camp with barbed wire fences and guards with machine guns located almost three thousand miles away near a town called Petawawa, Ontario.

Tomiko watched from her window. As she followed the truck down the road, she suddenly felt a strange tingling run up and down her legs. She bent down to rub the skin beneath her dress. She then stood up and walked a few steps to the eating table. *What kind of man steals from his own people? What kind of man hurts another so badly the victim may never fully recover? And what would have happened to me?* She trembled at the thought.

From the table, she picked up the letter she had been reading all morning. It came from a Kamloops hospital. Most of the sentences were blacked out by the censor, but the most important one was as clear as the day. An uneven hand had written, "Will you marry me?"

Tomiko looked toward the window and saw the truck just before it disappeared in the distance. She envisioned a cane, a wheelchair perhaps. Holding the letter to her breast, she gazed at the distant mountains and the horizon came into focus. She smiled.

Incident at Lemon Creek

Darkness settled thickly around the teenager like the muck of wet earth. Tree branches reached out to prick his skin. Translucent shafts of the moon pierced the shadows with a cold light, illuminating nothing.

The ground was uneven and the underbrush crackled with every step he took. His father had told him he would be nearby but had become invisible. He felt profoundly alone. The cold axe he carried numbed his bare hands. His legs grew heavy as lead. The lateness of the hour, the chill of the night and the urgency of purpose preyed on his mind, drawing him to the edge of fatigue, threatening to push him over into the depths of exhaustion.

A loud crack of dry wood sounded before him. He froze. Then a jigsaw piece of night shifted, and his mind raced with possibilities. "Lemon, is that you?" A rush of violent wind, the sudden prospect of certain death blasted against his face.

★

Lemon Ichikawa, a tall boy with a fresh face and hair slicked down, led the way stumbling over the jagged rock between the endless line of railroad ties. Tak Ogura, of Lemon's age and height but with long and unkempt hair, and Miki Hirano, at fifteen the youngest by three years, followed behind. The trio of friends gingerly walked between the Slocan and Valhalla ranges of the West Kootenay region of British Columbia. Lemon Creek flowed close by, leading back to the internment camp of rickety shacks constructed in neat rows, not far from its banks.

By the summer of 1942, the boys, their parents and hundreds of others had settled into the routine of waiting every morning for the crews of men to draw water from the creek and haul it by truck to camp. Then the day began. After taking their ration of water, the families could wash, cook, clean and bathe. The condition of the

121

crude toilets, thin walls and a chaotic mess hall tormented them, but a semblance of order existed. It masked a quiet desperation.

"That sun's plenty warm," Tak commented as he shielded his slitted eyes. His narrow jaw pulled his mouth into a grimace.

"Sure a lot better than last winter," Miki responded.

"Yeah, that was the worst!" Tak continued. "Nearly froze to death. My ma couldn't leave nothing on the stove. It always froze overnight!"

"Say, you fellahs hear about those two guys at Three Valley Gap?" Lemon interrupted.

Tak picked up a stray rock and heaved it at a bird in flight. "Who?"

"Two *nisei* guys."

"What about 'em?"

"I heard they died trying to escape."

"No fooling? How'd they die?"

"Fell in the water and drowned." Lemon picked up a rock and joined his friend.

"Did they find the bodies?" Miki asked. He licked the palm of his hand and began wetting down his cow-lick.

"Not that I know of." Lemon kicked at the ground, stirring up dust and pebbles. "You know, I can't blame 'em for trying to escape. A dollar a day digging out a highway. Not knowing what happened to their families. I'd give anything to get outta this hellhole myself."

"Where would you go?" Miki asked innocently.

"Anywhere I could get a job or go to school. I'm eighteen! I can't spend my life here!"

"You know what people are saying about us," Tak reminded. "Nobody wants us. *The New Canadian* said Kelowna didn't want any Japs dumped on them. Which is pretty funny since the town's full of Japs."

"What do you mean?"

"I mean it's the local Japs saying we shouldn't oughta come! They say they spent too much time building up their reputations for us to come along and spoil it."

"Yeah, well, so I don't go to Kelowna."

"But that goes for just about every city and town across the country."

Lemon's eyes flashed anger. "Listen, I'm getting out, see. No matter what it takes!"

The longing to escape obsessed Lemon. At night, the darkness comforted him by hiding the claustrophobic dimensions of the three-room shack, which held the three in his family and the Satos with their two toddlers. Privacy was not a concern. There simply wasn't any to be had. Only in his imagination could he feel the walls expanding to a silent space that gave him the time and emptiness to think.

He focused on the urgency to leave. There was nothing but a dead end for any eighteen-year-old in Lemon Creek. The army was the answer, but they weren't taking *enemy aliens* at the moment. Back in Vancouver, he had tried to enlist by changing his telltale name.

"What's your name, son?" asked the recruiting officer in China-town.

"Harry. Harry Chow. I live on East Pender," he offered, averting his eyes.

"I see," nodded the sombre-faced man with thick black-framed glasses. "I'm gonna need some ID, Harry."

He bent forward with an urgency, "Ah, can't we forget that? See, I'm willing and able to volunteer. I wanna fight the Japs."

"I know you do, son, but I can't take you in without ID. What if you were Japanese yourself? I'd be in a lot o'trouble then, wouldn't I?"

Lemon had motioned with understanding, shoved his hands in his pockets and turned to leave.

The same happened at every recruiting office in town. In the end, he went with his parents to Lemon Creek. Though his nickname came from his taste for lemonade and had nothing to do with the camp, he liked the coincidence. It gave him a certain sense of belonging. Still, he clung to the hope of joining the army as his way out, if only he could get to another province.

As he ruminated, he stared out the window, straight at the schoolhouse, a large one-room wooden building opposite his shack. Low lights burned from within, noticeable with nightfall. The roar of argument suddenly erupted, rumbling through the walls and across the grounds. Lemon opened the door and ran over to investigate.

At the side window, he strained his eyes to peer inside. All he could see were jagged shadows of men around a lamplit figure trembling in fear. Two men roughly grabbed their victim by the arms and pushed him out the door.

Lemon fell back on his haunches as he recognised the voices of Sasaki's *judō* boys from Vancouver, recruited by the *sonchō* for the purpose of intimidation. Fear tingled up his spine. He couldn't identify their prey but he felt sorry for him.

A flurry of hard slaps and cracks of wood broke the stillness of the night air. A confusion of shouts and screams culminated in the soft thud of a body. Lemon scrambled to the front of the building. He discovered a lump of flesh lying outside the schoolhouse. It was Kozai, the clerk in the grocery store! "Jesus, why him?" Lemon questioned out loud. He couldn't understand why they would bother with such an honest man. He bent down fearfully. Kozai didn't seem to be breathing, but Lemon couldn't tell unless he looked closer.

He fought the urge to gag when he saw that the body was oozing with blood. He felt his brow break out into a cold sweat. His hands began to tremble, his knees buckled. More shouts came from behind him, and instantly he bolted into the nearby trees.

A midnight tapping at the window. Moonlight streamed in and bathed the small, partitioned bedroom with a dull wash. Tak stirred in bed and woke with a start.

He pushed aside his wool blanket and slid out of the warmth into the cold night. Peering through the glass, he recognised his friend and opened the window.

Lemon stood chugging steam into the cold air. Beads of sweat filmed his troubled face. "Tak," he began, "you got any money I could have?"

"Money? What's happened, Lemon?"

"Can't tell ya. I gotta get outta here."

"Not that again. You can't escape. The Mounties will catch you for sure."

"I'm not worried about the Mounties. I've got to get away from here or I'm a *goner.*"

"What're you talking about?"

"I saw something," he said in a whisper.

"What?"

"I ... I saw a murder."

"What? Who?"

"Kozai-*san.* By the schoolhouse. They beat him and left him for dead."

"The grocer clerk? Who'd wanna kill him?"

"Sasaki."

"The *sonchō*? Why would the camp leader ...?"

"Listen, I've got no time to talk. I think they saw me. Can you help me out? Oh hell, I hear someone coming. Gotta go ..." Lemon receded into darkness.

Tak closed the window and withdrew. A confusion of shadow figures danced across the glass. Angry voices murmured just outside the window, shaking the frame slightly.

Everybody in Lemon Creek gathered at noon in the one-room schoolhouse for a town meeting. Reverend Komiyama stood tall at the front of the room, his long arms spread like wings floating on the agitated words of the crowd.

"Quiet everyone. Quiet!" he ordered in Japanese.

The voices subsided.

"Thank you. As you may already know, my son and I found Kozai, the grocer, badly beaten last night. He was lying unconscious in front of this building. Couldn't tell us anything. Officer Duggan took him to the hospital in Kamloops in his car." The room rumbled with concern and conjecture. "Also, Lemon Ichikawa has disappeared. The boy's mother came to me this morning pretty upset. Said her son hadn't slept in his bed and was nowhere to be found. I told her we'd do everything possible to find him. There are some questions I have ..."

"You think the boy beat up Kozai?" asked a *judō* man with a smirk.

The minister retorted quickly, "Let's just say the boy may know something."

Reverend Komiyama turned and pointed to a small man by the side wall with his arms folded over his protruding stomach. "Morishita-san, you say you saw the boy last?"

"Well yeah, sensei," he began, looking a bit startled. "I could've sworn I saw him walking outta camp last night."

"When was that?"

" 'Bout midnight ... No later. 'Bout one, maybe."

The crowd grew restless again. Tak Ogura stood near the back of the room, shuffling his feet, grinding his hands into one another. He tilted his head back in quiet debate with himself. Should he make his way to the front and tell all he knew? He looked at Isamu Sasaki, the *sonchō*, standing near Reverend Komiyama. The man's face was grim with a deep scar down the left side. The eyes glared intensely, never missing a nuance of expression on every face present. Sasaki was a man to be feared, a man never to be crossed.

"*Sa*," said the minister as he pulled at his sparse moustache. "Let's look for him!"

Sasaki gestured to his men to co-operate.

Tak joined his father, a rugged man with the iron arms and legs of a lumberjack, and four others in one of the search parties. Their task was to scour the woods beyond Anderson Hill, a grassy slope at the western edge of the camp.

They wore high boots and carried axes to clear underbrush. The trees were thick, their branches bent low with the weight of age. Shadows hung from the treetops and grew longer as the day crept towards evening.

As they moved into the darkness of the wood and night, each man lost track of the others. Tak strained his eyes to find his father. He thought he heard him rustling a few feet away but could not be sure.

Tak pulled his jacket tight, shivering from the cold. He breathed out a heavy steam as his thoughts turned to Lemon's fate. *There. A body slumped over a felled tree trunk. The head bashed in — the eyes gouged out. Blood turned brown in the light and oxygen. There, a body dead from exposure. Limbs broken and twisted from a terrible fall. Here. A body torn apart by predator claws. A look of absolute surprise on the face.*

A crack and a jigsaw piece of darkness moved in front of him. He froze. His lips began a silent tremble. My God, could it be? he whispered. His hands grew cold in their grip of the axe handle. "Lemon, is that you?"

An unearthly mass suddenly lunged toward him tearing at the fabric of the night. Sharp, jagged weapons sliced through the air heading straight for his heart. He couldn't move. Everything slowed in motion. He knew he was dead.

A flash of metal crossed his field of vision. Everything stopped. Tak crumpled to the ground. Before him lay the carcass of a deer, its blood streaming out of a wide gash to the head, flowing down its pelt and seeping into the ground. His father stood beside it inspecting the antlers. The axe held in his hands was stained with the blood of a fresh kill.

"Takeshi, you all right?" he said with concern in broken English.

All the search parties returned without finding anything. It was as if Lemon Ichikawa had disappeared off the face of the earth.

Mrs. Ichikawa stood shaking in her cabin as she listened quietly to
the minister.

"I'm sorry Ichikawa-san, but we'll keep up the search. Don't
worry, we'll find him." He felt the emptiness of his words even as
he said them.

Three days of looking, as expected, produced nothing. Everyone then left Mrs. Ichikawa alone, until the day weeks later she
burst out of her cabin, screaming. Reverend Komiyama immediately took her to his shack to calm her and sent for the B.C. Security Commission authorities. Late that evening, two men in grey
coats and hats took Mrs. Ichikawa away in a car, never to be seen
again.

Late summer, the mosquitoes hovered in the amber light of the
season. The time of *Obon*, the commemoration of the dead. Tak
and his parents petitioned for special passes to spend the day in Slocan City, seven miles from Lemon Creek, to visit friends and to
offer incense to ancestors during a service in the local cemetery.

By the graves of Japanese internees, the Buddhist minister chanted
the *sutra* that entreated lost relatives to return to loved ones, if only for
a day. Tak quietly chanted along, slowly mesmerised by the droning
spell. Suddenly, he was awake and alert. A gust of wind? A slight
movement of tree branches? He couldn't see anything unusual, yet a
presence was palpable.

That night during dinner, Tak could not concentrate on the
conversation. His mind constantly cast back to the cemetery.
When asked a courtesy question by his hosts, he muttered something absent-mindedly. His father thought him rude but everyone
else ignored him.

After dinner, he slipped away from his parents, who were en-
grossed in conversation with their friends, and headed for the cemetery, which lay like a shadow on the edge of town. The wooden
grave markers resembled the broken teeth of some menacing predator in the falling dark and ground mist.

The darkness crept toward blackness and mist flowed into wavering forms. Tak's eyes widened, his arms tingled with goose-bumps. A soft updraft swirled the transparent haze into a familiar shape. As he fell to his knees, he brought his hands together and stuttered through the *Nembutsu*.

Lemon Ichikawa's face, sallow and drawn, emerged from within the shape. He seemed to be floating in mid-air. What clothes could be seen were covered with mud. His body without legs.

"Tak." *It's the wind. The grass rustling.* "Don't be afraid. It's me, Lemon."

Still on his knees, Tak fought the urge to look.

"Listen to me. Yes I'm dead ... I'm not at peace. You've got to help me. Tak, you've got to."

Tak felt a coldness embrace his upper arms. He lifted his head. "It can't be. I'm dreaming."

"No. It's really me."

"What ... what happened?" the boy stammered as he rubbed warmth back into his arms.

"I'm buried in a shallow grave. You've got to get *sensei* to sanc-tify the grave. I can't be at peace." The ghost tilted his head to one side. The mist started to dissipate. "Help me ..."

"No! Wait, don't go! Lemon, were you murdered like you said? Lemon!" Too late. The image disappeared. Tak was alone once again in the cemetery. A warm wind dried his tears.

Reverend Komiyama stared at the young man before him. After a time, he found a simple way in Japanese to say what had to be said. "Takeshi, you were dreaming at the time."

"I thought so too, but no, *sensei*. It was Lemon. It really was." He answered in English.

"You know something about this Kozai business and Lemon's disappearance?"

"Who me? No, no not really." The boy lowered his head and kicked at the ground.

"You know Kozai is in pretty bad shape. No one knows if he'll walk again."

"Listen *sensei*, all I know is that you've got to do what Lemon asked. You don't have to believe me but please do it. Maybe not for Lemon's sake, but for his mom."

The minister saw the tears in the young eyes and nodded silently.

The next day, Reverend Komiyama stood at the edge of camp dressed in his black robe. He clapped his hands together and began to chant. Next to him, Tak lit incense. As the smoke curled, the aroma swirled about the air and conjured up the spirit of the Buddha. The minister performed the benediction.

> *We surround all men and all forms of life with Infinite Love and Compassion. Particularly do we send forth loving thoughts to those in suffering and sorrow; to all those in doubt and ignorance, to all who are striving to attain Truth; and to those whose feet are standing close to the great change men call death, we send forth oceans of Wisdom, Mercy and Love. Namu Amida Butsu. Namu Amida Butsu. Namu Amida Butsu.*

As the chanting faded into silence, Tak's anxieties dissipated. A warm wind rose and wrapped around his body as if to hug him. He closed his eyes. Somehow he knew Lemon's wish had been fulfilled. A deep sadness gradually overtook his euphoria as he realised he longed to see his friend one last time.

★

"Is that you Lemon?" In the silence Tak heard the words of fifty years ago.

The nursing home walls, painted green and washed down with alcohol, defined the boundaries of his night-world. Tak Ogura lay in his bed as stiff as a corpse, his face frozen in the slack-jaw aftermath of his latest stroke. On the night table, an ornate brass lamp with a frilly shade illuminated photographs of Canadian grandchildren playing in a suburban backyard, a wife, long ago dead, preparing their last New Year's feast, an old couple in sepia tones and turn-of-the-century Japanese attire and a cottage deep in a northern Ontario forest. Their frames boxed those moments neatly. The lamplight quietly flickered and went out. He didn't move. He couldn't move. The last of three strokes had completely paralysed him. But it really didn't matter. In darkness or in light, he didn't want to move. His muscles never even twitched as he faced the ghosts of his past alone.

The Brown Bomber

the chatter
          of never-closed mouths
the rain
               falls
endlessly

The grey dark figures circled one another drowning within the swirling static of a ten-inch screen. A tentative jab. A short sidestep. A quick step in — a lightning left hook. The opponent buckled and collapsed with a thud. The champ raised his arms in victory.

She sat on the edge of an overstuffed sofa, her left foot tapping out the seconds that piled into minutes that slouched toward the hour. The front room, cluttered with Japanese wall hangings, religious books and ornate used furniture, pressed in on her. She paid little attention to the television, her ears attuned to the arrival of her fiancé's Chevrolet.

"Joe Louis, the Brown Bomber, has won!" declared the television announcer. The crowd roared, "Brown Bomber! Brown Bomber!" The chanting pulled her back to the screen.

What began as dabs of wetness in the corners of her eyes flooded into sobbing. She reached for the tissue on the veneered coffee table before her. Mascara ran like hot tar down her face. She fingered the packed valise at her feet to remind her of Frank, the man who would take her away from this existence.

She indelicately blew her nose and promptly left the room. The clicking of half-heels rushed across the wooden floor and up the stairs. The narrow bathroom at the top landing reflected her mother's financial state and lack of taste: worn pink tile and an odds-and-sods collection of towels.

She scolded herself as she looked into the chrome-edged mirror. Her broad face with full red lips stared back. She noted the laugh lines, the hint of jowls under her jawline. Her eyes puffy from crying, her cheeks molten mounds of red.

Shameful, she thought as she cupped cold water to wash her face. *Crying over such a foolish thing!* She gasped for air as she reached for the frayed green face-cloth next to the flowered bath towel. As she wiped away the tears and cosmetic mud, she inspected her skin.

She rubbed the surface in a vain effort. "I'm not so dark," she tried to reassure herself. The walls closed round conspiratorially as she steadied herself against the cool half-basin.

★

Kimiko Matsuba looked to the sky and the mounting clouds above the thick forest. The unseen forces of war had driven her family from Vancouver to the small shanty-town camp near a river bank in the middle of the mountains. The swollen waters warned of an approaching storm.

She lived with her parents in a shack at the end of Row D in the Lemon Creek internment area. They shared the close quarters with the Kiyonaga family – Buddhists who were part of the overflow sent from Sandon camp. The B.C. Security Commission was beginning to see the impracticality of imprisoning the Japanese Canadians by religion.

Until recently, Kimiko's father, Toshiro, had been with a road gang somewhere in the Interior. He had managed to obtain permission from the authorities to rejoin his family shortly after they arrived in Lemon Creek.

Before the war, Toshiro Matsuba had roved the countryside as an itinerant labourer in search of employment. He was a tall man with prominent cheek-bones and large hands that possessed a surprisingly gentle touch. A quiet man, he never complained about the gruelling work found in the copper mines, sawmills and lumber camps.

His mouth remained tightly closed even as they took him from his Vancouver home in the middle of the night shortly after the Japanese bombed Pearl Harbor, a place unknown to him.

He stood before his kidnappers – sullen, his eyes turned down, as if he half-expected his fate.

"Tojiro Matba," the seated man in a suit addressed him. "Hell, we'll call you *Tojo* for short."

Toshiro said nothing, not even to correct his name.

"You're what we consider to be an *Enemy Alien*. You're going to

be part of a gang building a road." Another man in shadows snig-
gered. "Well *Tojo*, what do you think of that?"

Toshiro thought of his wife and daughter but stayed silent. He felt
the strength drain from his arms, the resolve in his heart dissipate.

"Christ, another one that don't know English!" The official motioned to his subordinate to take the prisoner away.

Kimiko, a pretty girl of sixteen with wide brown eyes, fleshy hips
and a dark complexion, did not understand what had befallen her
father, who only two weeks before had made his way home from a
lumber camp to Vancouver when the news broke about Pearl Harbor. She saw her mother wither with worry during the days following the midnight arrest. Two men in grey coats at the door had
simply ordered Toshiro to come with them. *Otōsan* looked at
mother; *okāsan* looked at father. Fear and resignation flooded their
faces. Then he was gone.

No one knew where. It seemed, Kimiko discovered, every
able-bodied man was torn from his home in the same manner. The
authorities were deaf to questions by family members. Instead
what followed in rapid succession was the closing of community
newspapers, language schools and churches. A curfew was im-
posed. Travel passes cancelled.

Kimiko carried on as best she could in the face of restricted
movement orders and her mother's bouts of panic and loneliness.
At high school, she pretended nothing was different. She studied
her arithmetic. She read her Shakespeare. She joked with friends.
She withstood the usual taunts.

"Hey Brown Bomber!"

"Don't call me that!" she scolded.

Freddy Yoshida laughed and ran down the hall.

She turned away embarrassed. Gracie and Midge caught up to
her. "What'd Freddy say to you?"

She stood still, mute and diminished. She touched her skin. Her
two friends saw her shudder and changed the subject. "I heard we
won't be in school by Easter vacation," informed Midge.

"On account of the war," Gracie added as she adjusted her
wire-rimmed glasses.

"What do you mean?"

"I mean they're gonna close the school down just like the language schools and newspapers," Midge explained. "'Cause we're all Japanese here."

Kimiko felt a chill, a creeping paralysis.

"Brown Bomber! Brown Bomber!" The shouts echoed off the institutional green walls as Freddy and Billy whizzed by the trio.

"Shutup, you *bakatare*! C'mere and I'll sock you one!" Midge threatened, her fist raised. Her stout body shook with anticipation. She met only a rain of laughter as the boys escaped to a grade ten math class.

Kimiko slumped into a dark silence.

Home was no sanctuary. Haruko Matsuba, a gaunt woman with flattened breasts and curveless body, rattled around the rooms looking for things to do. Her thin-lipped mouth, creased at the corners with worry, tightened at the thought of penury. She was used to her husband's long absences but not without a paycheque.

Haruko cluttered the kitchen to mask the need for food money. She stuffed the tattered, the worn and the old into closets. She covered the rips of her Victorian couches with material. All in an effort to keep poverty and pity at bay. Still, she felt compelled to do more.

Take in more laundry. Take in more sewing. Clean houses. What could she do without Toshiro? She wrapped herself in her tapered bone-thin arms.

Kimiko waited every evening in the public library until a half-hour before curfew to go home. In her usual carrel, she read the various Vancouver newspapers that were filled with the words of politicians in Victoria and then Ottawa. Their speeches called for the banishment of the trouble-makers, saboteurs and Japs in general from the coast. Day after day, the accusations, the epithets and demands mounted until the pages were filled with them. Kimiko tried to distance herself from the rhetoric, but she knew something more was about to happen to them.

By late spring, Haruko and Kimiko were on their way to Lemon Creek. They hated to leave without *otōsan*, but there was no choice.

Their assigned shack held mean furniture, cracked chairs and table, and four bare bed frames. Rodent droppings were everywhere. Fine dust rose from the floor, clinging to the bottoms of their cotton dresses like the light grip of invisible hands.

Fresh water was brought in by trucks every morning, since Lemon Creek itself was just far enough away to make hauling water from it a Herculean task. Haruko sent Kimiko with a couple of buckets to wait in line at the truck. When her daughter returned, she could start making breakfast, doing the wash or scrubbing the floor.

While she waited, Kimiko heard the taunts once again. "Hey Brown Bomber! *Kuro-chan, kuro-chan*! You're a dirty Negro baby." Young kids bobbed and weaved in and about the line, jeering all the while. No one shouted a rebuke. All eyes turned away. Kimiko's own eyes trembled but not in self-pity or hurt. Her dress would never be free of the dust, she thought.

★

She could hear the television set muttering downstairs. The narrator explained how Joe Louis – the Dark Destroyer, the Sepia Slugger, the accursed Brown Bomber – had reigned over the heavyweight boxing world for twelve years, longer than anyone. The viewers had just relived the victorious moment twenty-two years ago when the Brown Bomber knocked out the former champion and Nazi symbol Max Schmeling in the 1938 rematch bout.

Using the mirror, Kimiko carefully lined her eyes with the mascara stick. The dams were redrawn. The tears held within the reservoir.

She puffed up her hairdo with a comb, checked her lipstick and adjusted her blouse and jacket before re-entering the dark hallway. She had never liked the atmosphere of the house. Too suffocating, she complained. Her heels noisily led her down the linoleum-covered steps. Her tight skirt rasped against her nylons. In the front room, she quickly switched off the offensive program.

She sat down, thought about lighting a cigarette, but decided

against it. This was her mother's house still. She thought it funny or
perhaps a little shameful that she could be so easily distracted by the
television when she really should be thinking about her future.
Then again there was the question of her future with Frank. Uncertain. One day at a time, she advised herself.

The bric-a-brac on nearby tables caught her attention. The
wooden Japanese figurines; the ceramic *bonsai* (the real ones were
too expensive); the *daruma*, its one eye blind, its wish unfulfilled: all
spoke of contemporary Japan. Relatives had sent them as emis-
saries in an effort to keep in touch, as proof of their slow but pro-
gressive recovery. There wasn't anything of the war or prior to the
war, except two enlarged wall photographs in oval wooden frames.
The figures sat in the traditional austere pose of the last century.
Draped in great formal *kimono*, the couple stared past the camera
(Kimiko imagined) without expression: lifeless eyes, down-turned
mouths and pallid skin. Grandparents. Anonymous, yet the family
resemblance was unmistakable. Father's high cheek-bones.

★

About two weeks after Haruko and her daughter came to Lemon
Creek, Toshiro joined them. Kimiko felt a renewed security the day
he returned, but she noticed that something had changed in him.
His eyes had taken on a haunted look.

Otōsan said nothing about his disappearance, and his wife and
daughter knew better than to ask. When he removed his shirt, he
looked a little frail, the rib-cage sharply defined. Both women
gasped at the dried gash along his left arm. Haruko quickly pulled
Kimiko toward the table.

"We can cook otōsan a good meal now," she said, gathering the
vegetables.

Back within the bosom of family, Toshiro let worry slip away.
Life wasn't too bad anymore. Better than being a couple of hundred miles into the bush, clearing land and grading road.

He heard of an *ofuro* over at Slocan City. Hot reviving water and cleansing steam appealed to him. With special permission, a refugee towel and frayed *yukata*, he began the seven-mile walk to Slocan.

In about two hours, he reached the small settlement. He ignored the accusing scrutiny of the white townspeople as he sauntered along the dusty road to the internment area on the edge of town. He was about to be treated to a healing bath.

The shacks looked the same as those in Lemon Creek, just more of them. Rows and rows of them. Laundry hung on makeshift lines. Young men idled outside while their mothers, grandmothers and sisters scrubbed and washed.

In the distance by the shores of Lake Slocan, Toshiro noticed a solitary cabin with a long queue of internees in front of it. The chatter of Japanese swarmed above the crowd like summer gnats. He soon joined the line.

"Say, what's going on?" Toshiro asked the closest man.

The bent man with wispy white hair and river-bed hands pulled his robe tight. "Ofuro is pretty busy."

"How long is the wait?"

"Oh about two hours."

"Two hours!"

The old man raised his eyebrows. "You have something else to do?"

The Slocan *ofuro* was a disappointment to Toshiro. With the long wait, his expectations grew high, but the crudely fashioned barrels sweating with condensation were rough to the touch. He imagined invisible slivers penetrating his skin as he slipped into the tub. The water was hot enough, but with continuous use, a layer of scum had formed on the surface. He soon gave up his spot in the tub and took the first steps of the lonely trip home.

Back at the Lemon Creek internment camp, Toshiro convinced the men to build an *ofuro* of their own. They liked the idea of something to do and relished the thought of a luxurious bath in the middle of this godforsaken wilderness. Some even chuckled over constructing something so Japanese given their predicament.

Working enthusiastically, Toshiro and a crew of four took just three days to build their *ofuro*. The small, crude shack stood on the banks of Lemon Creek to take advantage of the easy access to water. The lumber and tarpaper came from scraps of discarded government supplies used for the construction of the camp's family dwellings.

Building leak-proof soaking tubs proved to be the main challenge. The men collected wooden staves from broken barrels, reshaped them and strung them together with wire. Toshiro melted tar and applied it between the staves. As a result, a heavy, choking smell lingered.

Toshiro, as the innovator and project leader, was given the honour of being first to use the *ofuro*. As he washed himself from a bucket of cold water, men filled the tubs with water heated over an open fire outside.

Toshiro tentatively tested the bath with his foot. The others watched in anticipation. He faked a pained expression and then winked at his audience. His body sank into the pool until the water was up to his chin. The crowd cheered as he sighed contentedly.

★

As she looked at her grandparents' portraits, Kimiko recalled her childhood suspicion that she was not related to her parents. Her father bore the family resemblance. She did not. Her mother was skinny with thin lips and slender limbs. She was not. She considered herself a "full figure woman" as in the Wonder Bra commercials. Her hair was thick, easy to curl. Both parents had sparse, faded hair.

It was her skin that linked her to her mother. Haruko's complexion was ruddy, a natural reddish brown deepened by the massaging rays of the sun. Kimiko had inherited the same dark skin.

"Why am I so dark?" whined Kimiko as a child to her mother.

"Because you are my daughter," she answered in Japanese.

"What does that mean?"

"It means you are the granddaughter of a farmer in Japan. He worked in the sun all day long."

"I'm not a farmer," she complained. "The kids all say I must be a negro!"

"*Ahō!*" Haruko admonished. Her eyes flickered red. "You are not kuro-chan. You are Japanese! Always remember that."

She never did forget that scolding and the others like it. Being Japanese, however, did not offer her much escape from community persecution. The skin, her damn skin. Cruel, ignorant boys ridiculed her, girls pitied her, adults scorned her behind her back.

She felt a guilty yet delicious sensation deep in her being the day after Pearl Harbor. At least she knew they were all in the same boat. The boys, the girls, the people in the shops and homes could not escape the fact that they were all Japanese. They could no more remove their faces than she could rub off the colour of her skin.

To her surprise, the derision and teasing continued.

★

In her most private moments Kimiko wept quietly. The moonlight streamed through the crude square of a window. The underside of clouds on the horizon shimmered.

She sat by the window late at night while the Kiyonaga children slept. The adults lay in bed as well but she couldn't tell if all were asleep. Her father usually snored deeply. No one would have attempted to comfort her anyway. It was not their way.

Random thoughts ran through her mind. Even in camp, they called her Brown Bomber. It seemed preposterous given the enormity and implications of their situation. She shook her head. *We're all in the same boat here. A Jap is a Jap. Maybe they need to pick on me ... to make me be a kuro-chan ... to feel better about being here.* Her mind flashed to the day in 1937 when Joe Louis first captured the heavyweight title.

"Hey, did you hear the Brown Bomber did it?"

"What's a *brown bomber*?" Kimiko asked innocently.

Tom Ohara grimaced and pushed back his bangs. "What? You never heard of Joe Louis, the Brown Bomber, the Dark Destroyer, the Sepia Slugger? He's the new heavyweight champion of the world!"

"Champion of what?"

"Boxing!" He crossed his arms and smirked at the other three who had gathered in the school hallway.

"Oh. But why is he called the *Brown Bomber*?"

"Oh brother, are you stupid or what?" Kimiko grew angry. Tom headed off her objections. "'Cause he's a Negro, ya goof."

The circle in the school hallway broke into laughter.

"What's so funny?" she complained.

"'Cause you don't know nothing."

It wasn't long after that she herself became known as the Brown Bomber. Her ignorance and her complexion made the connection a natural. Close friends, Grace Ohtani and Midge Tanaka, stood by her and challenged her persecutors. They could not, however, stop the wild flock of children from swarming around her in Powell Grounds, mocking her with the nickname.

At Lemon Creek she didn't even have the respite Grace and Midge had offered. They had been evacuated to some place called Kaslo.

Father began to snore. She sat by the window for hours thereafter, her thoughts and handkerchief her only company. She recalled the newspapers and heard the words of the politicians in the B.C. Legislature and Parliament condemning her, her family, her friends for being born. *Maybe they need to pick on me but I feel alone.*

*

As she sat in front of the blank television set, she felt the emotion well up again. Her stomach sank; her heart pumped harder to counter the flood. She was thinking of Roy, her first love, the man who could have taken her to the suburbs, given her children, allowed her into the stream of normal community conversation.

Roy Sunada was not a handsome man. His broad, flat nose

punctuated the rough, unfinished look of his face. His short, stocky stature contributed to his lack of appeal since most *nisei* women who had resettled in Toronto after the war felt a man should be taller than his girlfriend.

On the other hand, the *issei* parents considered him a good catch for their daughters. He was industrious. He had left his family in Slocan and ventured to Toronto, one of the first to arrive after the war. He faked a name and worked in Chinese laundries until he learned enough to start a dry-cleaning business of his own in the early 1950s.

Kimiko met him at a *nisei* dance held at the Ukrainian Hall on Bathurst Street. She was persuaded to attend the monthly Saturday night dance by her old friends Grace and Midge, who had come to Toronto shortly before her.

"Hey doll face, you wanna dance?" Roy asked as the band moved into "In the Mood." He slicked back his hair and offered his hand.

"No, you don't wanna dance with me," she answered with a self-conscious smile. "Ask my friend Gracie." Grace Ohtani pushed her friend as encouragement.

"I want you, sugar," he insisted. "I ain't asking twice."

She surprised herself with her sudden flight to the dance floor. The rocking and jiving of a jitterbug step seemed as natural to her as if she were in the hands of a professional.

★

The popularity of the *ofuro* was instant and widespread throughout the internment camp. As in Slocan, long lineups soon formed. To keep a constant supply of clean hot water available, a rotating committee of internees stoked the fire under the pots by the river while patrons quietly waited to enjoy the rejuvenating bath. The building accommodated four people at a time.

"I'm not going in there," complained Kimiko in Japanese.

"And why not?" Haruko retorted.

"What if a man comes in?"

"So?"

"Well, he'll see me!" She had become self-conscious of her budding figure.

"Ahō. What do you think will happen? Most of the men around here are too old and the young ones aren't interested in you. That skin of yours."

Kimiko fell silent. The blunt words shocked her. The irony confused her. Wasn't her mother's complexion like hers? Her mother insisted she was Japanese yet she was not, because of her skin. Her fate was sealed. She guessed she would never marry and find happiness.

★

"No!" Kimiko complained. "I'm not that kind of girl." The cliché tumbled out of her mouth as she pushed Roy's hand away.

"Ah c'mon, sugar. I love you," grumbled Roy as he ensnared a breast.

Kimiko's girlfriends couldn't see the attraction. This five-foot-four, somewhat crude man had the appeal of dirty dishes in a sink. On the dance floor, they looked like Mutt and Jeff. Kimiko stood five-foot-eight in heels. They gambolled around the room, bumping into other couples, tables and chairs.

Attitudes shifted as the relationship developed. Midge said he must be a nice guy since he had shown up with flowers on the first date. And once Grace heard that Kimiko was helping out as bookkeeper and counter person at the dry-cleaners, she agreed that Roy had potential.

Kimiko looked around the one-room flat above the business. Her cliché protestations had melted and were swept away by pleasure. *But it isn't right. I should wait.* The furnishings cried out for a woman's touch, she thought as she closed her eyes. *What does it matter?* She was aware of Roy below.

She opened her eyes and chose to look to the simple desk, the chair, the hotplate, the icebox, the piles of *Popular Mechanics* magazines, the floral bedspread. From his mother, no doubt. She accommodated a new position.

Her ears glowed hot. Sweat rose on her skin. As her imagination soared, she broke into a smile. Her rapture blocked out the fevered grunting, blinded her to the contorted face moving above her.

★

The night grew long as the moon waned. Kimiko continued to look through the shack window but was lost in thought. She could never be close to her father. His silence kept him aloof. She complied with his wishes but could never break through his stoicism.

Faint moonlight spilled from behind the rising bank of clouds. She felt the far off rumble of thunder against her chest. She tasted moisture in the air.

Toshiro's snores stuttered to a stop. He rolled away from his wife and came to his feet on the rough-hewn floor. He turned to the sound of quiet weeping.

"Kimi-chan," he whispered softly, "why are you crying?"

Surprised, she twisted toward the window and hid her face within a handkerchief.

"Why are you crying?" he repeated.

She said nothing as she tried to stifle her hiccups for air.

He stood beside her. He moved to stroke her ample hair but stopped short. "Kimi-chan, life is not so bad. Things have a way of working themselves out." Her eyes turned down in the pale window light. He whispered in English. "Some-day we go. Then you marry."

★

Things have a way of working out. Her Japanese wasn't all that good but she had understood her father that night. *Otōsan* believed in perseverance, sticking to it. That was how he built the *ofuro*. And

he had been right about the family. They had stuck out the deprivation of a prison camp, exile and oppression, and here they were
three thousand miles away in Toronto, mother and daughter, enjoying the security of a job and self-respect. *Poor otōsan*. Things had
worked out for the most part. Even the name-calling had become
an unpleasant memory, seldom remembered. "Roy," she whispered
as she reached across the bed.

In the years immediately following the war, Haruko and Kimiko
came to Toronto and struggled to find money for rent and food.
Haruko cleaned people's houses and took in sewing. Once in a
while, she wept silently.

Kimiko managed to take a night-school secretarial course and
found a decent job as a secretary for a Jewish clothing manufac-
turer. She took comfort in her father's last words to her – it was
1952 and she had found a good man.

"Roy," she called as she rose to a half-sitting position. She ruffled
the sheets to cover her bare skin from the cold. "Roy, can I talk to
you?"

"Yeah sure," he answered as he lit up a cigarette by the icebox.

"Roy, can I ask you something?"

He emerged through a plume of smoke, clad in his boxer shorts
and striking a casual pose by the bed. "What is it?" he grunted.

"We've been … um … dating about a year now." She folded her
lower lip beneath her teeth. "We know each other really well." She
flushed a faint shade of red. Her hands pulled the sheets to her
tighter. "We get along."

"What're you trying to say?" he growled in a defensive tone.

She sucked in a breath of air. "I think we should get married,"
she blurted. Roy turned his back to her. Smoke rose above him.
"Sugar, this is how it is." He faced her again. "Fact is, I ain't ready.
The business is struggling, see."

"Oh Roy, you think I care about that? The business is not that
bad off. I can quit my job and help you full-time. We can make a
real go of it!"

"Yeah, that's fine, fine, but I'm not the kind of guy you wanna
marry." He covered his eyes to protect them from her gaze.

"Don't be silly. It's my idea, remember?"

He averted his head. His voice lowered. "I can't marry you."

"What?"

"I said I can't marry you."

The words jabbed. Fear seeped into her stomach. "Why not?"

"'Cause ... 'cause I'm already engaged."

Her face collapsed. Her weight fell away.

"I'm already engaged," he repeated, "to Sumi. Sumi Nagano. Last month."

Her eyes, her lips, her tightening jaw asked why.

"I couldn't marry you anyway. You see, you're too dark skinned. My *okāsan* told me you're not good enough. You know, not clean. How would it look? Hey, you said it yourself – I've got loads of potential. I've got my future to think about."

Kimiko heard the run-on of words, the schoolyard taunts, the camp catcalls.

★

With the dawn, the threat of a storm increased for Lemon Creek. The river churned angrily, desperate to leave the confines of bank and rock. Wind teased and tore at trees. Heavy clouds lowered.

Toshiro stepped gingerly into the still hot bath water. He was alone. The approaching storm had driven everyone away, even the fire stokers. Toshiro didn't care. What was a little rain? Were they afraid of getting wet after a bath? Ridiculous.

The river took on a slate grey colour. He shivered involuntarily at the wind driving the sudden rain like needles into the wall of the shack. Some great beast could be heard growling at a distance, and it was coming closer.

The hot water swirled around and massaged his tired muscles. He drifted in his thoughts and dreamed the roar of rushing water and the cracking of wood. When the *ofuro* caved in, he awoke before the heavy push of water swept everything away in a flash flood.

★

"It's settled, Mother. I am going to marry Frank." Kimiko stood defiant.

Her mother shook with anger. "You not marry!" she thundered in staccato English.

Kimiko held her ground. Her facial muscles constricted, her arms crossed her bosom tightly. "Look, I'm more than old enough to make my own decisions!"

"Kimiko, you should listen to your okāsan," whined Mrs. Takehara, the plump neighbour invited as an ally to common sense. "Marriage is an important step. You'll have to live with it for the rest of your life."

Kimiko's mind boiled with contempt. Who was this meddlesome woman always butting into other people's business? She wanted to scream.

"Think of your children," Haruko demanded, switching languages. "What are they going to look like? Half Japanese, half ..." The words caught in her throat.

"Negro, Mother! Frank is a Negro!"

Mrs. Takehara moved between them. Her ample build, soft features and concerned voice calmed the quarrel momentarily.

"Kimiko, the children *are* a consideration."

"How will you live?" Haruko erupted. "Where will you live?" She spat as she thought of the implications of proximity.

"New York. People don't care who marries who there! Frank's a jazz musician."

Haruko scoffed.

"He'll get gigs and I'll get a job."

The two older women dared not look at each other. They didn't understand English words like "jazz" and "gig," but they guessed at the life of a musician.

Mrs. Takehara paused and stood back before declaring, "I think you should marry your own kind."

"It doesn't matter what you think." She shifted her weight toward her mother. "I will marry Frank."

Haruko couldn't look at her. "You will bring shame to me and to the memory of your dead father."

The Japanese was clear. Kimiko shook, undecided what to do next.

★

The rain laughed steadily at the debris of the *ofuro* and tragedy. Several men had come running at the first sound of the crash.

"Matsuba-san!" cried one. "Matsuba-san was in there!"

Japanese voices and speculation arced high in the air.

"There's nothing left ... Must've been a huge wave ... Yeah, I saw it ... Like a tsunami ..."

Kimiko tried to break through the barrier of arms and bodies. The raging river swirled over its muddy banks. The brown waters dared anyone to approach.

She stopped, suddenly exhausted by the struggle.

"There's nothing left down there ... We'll set up a search party after ... go back ... take care of your mother ... Kiyonaga-san, help her ..."

The torrential rain pounded against her as Kimiko struggled to reach their shack. She knew *otōsan* was gone. No search party would ever find him. The strong, swift current obliterated everything in its path and carried the debris deep into the wild terrain. She whimpered into her already saturated sleeve, increasingly aware of the irony of her father's last words to her.

★

Things will work out. Frank Johnson was an itinerant musician trying to make it in a world wholly against his kind, playing a music few cared for and even fewer understood. Still Kimiko could see in his half-drawn eyes and barracuda smile the love he possessed for jazz and the rapture he found playing it.

She'd met him in one of those coffee-houses after-hours, when the bohemians and suburbans who aspired to be bohemian gathered for espresso and Kerouac.

The Japanese Canadians were given the vote in 1949, but it took Midge Tanaka nearly ten years before she started to enjoy democracy. When she did, she turned hipster and took to reading the beat poets and wearing black. The words were liberating. Work at the dress factory filled her days; coffee, jazz and smoke carried her through the night. She convinced Kimiko, her workmate and friend, to come with her to see how the less conventional lived.

Frank lumbered over to their table, saxophone slung around his neck. He extended his mitt of a hand to welcome Midge.

"Nice to see you again," he purred, the smile widening. "Say, who's your pretty friend?"

Kimiko blushed and offered her white-gloved hand. She became aware of her flower-print dress and white pumps. Altogether not "with it," she thought self-consciously.

Frank turned away, hoping his features hadn't scared her.

★

Kimiko heard the honking outside. She leaped to her feet, picking up the valise in the same motion. Through the front window, she saw Frank waving to her. The used gold Chevrolet, paid for with her savings, gleamed in the sun. In a few minutes they would be leaving Toronto, off to New York via a Justice of the Peace somewhere near Buffalo.

She felt the house drain empty as she walked outside. The last moments with her mother rushed back to her.

"I will not be home when that kurombo comes," Haruko hissed.

"All right, Mother," she responded dryly.

Mrs. Takehara stepped forward. Concern covered her face like rain on a window. "Kimiko-san, why do you want to marry a Negro?"

"Why? Why? Because everybody I've ever known says I look like one. So why shouldn't I marry one?"

The two *issei* women fell silent.

Kimiko greeted her fiancé without words. She could hear the chorus of voices rising in the school hallway, the camp grounds, the community buildings, the houses.

"Kuro, kuro, kuro-chan! Of course she married one. Look how dark the mother is. Brown Bomber! Brown Bomber!"

The voices soon mixed with the cries of opportunistic politicians in a verbal soup of name-calling, epithets, demands for exile, for confiscation, for imprisonment. Kimiko breathed a sigh of relief as the golden car pulled away, headed for a destination out of the country.

Only the Lonely

Roy Orbison sang quietly in the corner of the hotel room. The music was low; his voice plaintively high. Kay Ogawa sat unmoved on the edge of the tightly made bed. Her short legs, positioned one in front of the other, were adorned with white hose and black heels appropriate for her middle-class station in life. Her tiny hands waited, folded on her lap. Every silver strand of her neat coiffure remained in place. No earrings or necklaces, costume or otherwise. Her oval face, sullen in thought, featured a dull red lipstick, faint mascara and enough foundation to allow only a few telltale signs of her senior years to stand out – liver spots and shaded pouches of fat under the eyes.

As the radio played, she gradually indulged in introspection. She just didn't understand why she was there. She felt more than a little foolish and sad.

The Toronto skyline, through the window, seemed hard-edged despite the flickering lights and the soft rainfall. Sirens screamed deep in the belly of the city: the undercutting of a happy occasion. Life had changed so much since the time of her youth. Her two children were grown and out of the house, both living in Vancouver with prosperous careers. Her husband had recently died of cancer, but he had been a good man, providing well for his family. Things could have been a lot worse.

The music ended. The radio paused and then Roy Orbison sang again, the same song, at the same volume. She noticed the anomaly for a moment but then sank into her thoughts again. She held onto the chorus and saw the flow of her life in her mind's eye.

★

During the 1940s, the interior of British Columbia during April was miserable with rain. Moisture seeped into the bones, sending chills up the spine until even the head felt congested. Surrounding

157

mountains cut the sky with jagged heights. Their coats of evergreen swayed to the prodding winds. The cold spring humidity and precipitation gave no hope of any warm and hospitable weather to come.

In the spring of 1946, Japanese Canadians still remained within the confines of their prisons but were making plans for the future. Keiko "Kay" Ogawa, a teacher working at the Pine Crescent School in the Bayfarm internment area just outside Slocan City, unfolded a letter from a good friend, with some anticipation. She hadn't heard from her in a while.

April 16, 1946

Dear Kay,

Rain, rain, rain! That's all we seem to be having. I'm sure Roseberry is no better than where you are. We had a dance the other night. Shig Tanabe (you know Shig, the tall one with the funny nose?) brought out his old records and all us young people danced the night away in the Community Hall in New Denver. "Moonlight Serenade" was dreamy as I swirled around the floor to the music. Isn't life wonderful?

I spend most of my time teaching as you know. I miss the tête-à-têtes we had during our courses three summers ago. Remember? Say, when are you coming this way? Make it soon okay? My parents are talking about repatriating to Japan. I don't want to go. I'm a Canadian, not Japanese. Isn't that why our boys fought the war? I really think Ottawa is wrong in doing this to us. If anything, I choose moving east of the Rockies!

Write soon, okay?

Yours truly,
Fuzzy

Fusae sounded her old self except for the tone of trepidation. Kay knew the end of the war was no reason to celebrate for her friend, given her family's uncertain future. Her father was in a bad way. Parkinson's. The decision to go to Japan meant Fuzzy had to go as well. A daughter's compliance and help were expected. Still, Kay liked her friend's sense of hope expressed in the line: "Isn't life wonderful?"

★

The two friends had written to each other infrequently through-out the war, but they were always in each other's thoughts. They had met in the internment area of Slocan City after being persuaded by Sugimoto *sensei* to teach the internee children. They took the hastily fashioned courses during the summer of '43 to get some inkling of teaching fundamentals. What they also gained, before they separated for Roseberry and Bayfarm in September, was a friendship which the two knew would last a lifetime.

Each had some high-school education, grade eleven to be exact, when the war broke out. Keiko had argued that she knew nothing about teaching. The church-appointed Supervisor of Education insisted that she was needed.

"Keiko," explained Sugimoto *sensei*, "we can't let our young people run around and do nothing! They need an education. They need you."

Keiko stole a look at the expectant face of Hide Sugimoto, a *ni-sei* and the only accredited teacher in the entire Japanese Canadian community.

"I'm not a teacher," Keiko insisted.

"Yes, but you speak English well and you have the knowledge that the young need. That's the beginning of teaching!"

She finally agreed.

Fortunately, the classes she taught never gave her reason to regret her decision. The bright faces of her students looked up at her day in and day out with enthusiasm.

The boys wore smiles made broad by their close-cut hair. Some were *yancha*, getting into mischief all the time, but Keiko didn't mind. Tommy Tokunaga, a rough-and-tumble kid who wore his bruises like badges, sauntered into the one-room schoolhouse after class on a spring day with a bunch of flowers for her.

"*Sensei*, these are for you," he said with exaggerated motion of head and outstretched arm.

"Why Tommy, these are beautiful! Thank you," she answered while accepting the slightly damaged crocuses. "But why?"

He turned away shyly.

"Tommy?" She leaned forward.

The boy suddenly spun around and kissed her on the cheek. Keiko reared back, caught off guard. The equally startled student jerked up the belt of his blue jeans and scrambled out of the room.

The girls were different. No matter what, they wore clean, pretty dresses. Despite the dust, the poor conditions in camp, they always tried to look their best. Every one seemed to have bangs over her eyes and hair trimmed at the shoulders. Their faces were scrubbed and kneesocks pulled up tight. Smart too. Keiko knew they would never have trouble after the war.

"Sachiko, why did you do Frankie Kakuno's homework for him?" Keiko asked in a stern voice.

"Well, I really didn't ..." The young girl squeezed her hands into fists.

"There's no use denying it. I know Frankie's not capable of the work shown here."

"*Sensei*, it's not his fault. You see, he's from *inaka*."

"What's that got to do with anything?"

"He didn't get much school there. He had to be out in the fields a lot, helping his father with the crops and everything."

Keiko abruptly stopped mid-thought. Her face slowly itched with a slight embarrassment. *Everyone's in the same boat. No one thinks himself better or worse than the others. Good kids.* "Okay. Okay. Next time let him do his own work, *ne*? How is he going to learn anything otherwise?"

"Yes, *sensei*," she replied as she lowered her eyes to the floor.

★

Kay folded the letter into her dress pocket. *The war is over. Time to visit old friends*, she thought.

Four days later, she took the late-morning bus from Slocan City to New Denver, then walked the short distance to Roseberry. As in her camp, the slap-dash wooden shacks were the worse for wear. She recalled the particularly severe winters. In '42, the wind ripped right through the walls, freezing everything in its path, even the green sap bleeding out of her shack's two-by-four planks. When it fell, the deep snow was actually a relief since it acted as a wind block.

She slowed her pace when she caught sight of Fuzzy. On the porch stood a tall, skinny woman with her black hair in the tight curls of a permanent. Her dress hid her feet and a heavy wool coat covered her upper body. As Kay moved closer, she saw the familiar droop of the eyes, the bright whiteness of her friend's complexion and the too-long arms attached to oversized hands.

"Look at you!" squealed Kay as she enmeshed her fingers in the curls of hair.

"Me? How about you? You never did like long hair."

They embraced. Fuzzy's arms around Kay's head were almost suffocating but she didn't protest in the warmth of the moment.

Many had made fun of their difference in height, but the two friends hadn't cared. They simply smiled at each other. And so they smiled again as they walked to the edge of the camp before following the railroad tracks to the lake.

"Hey, Kay, remember this one?" Fuzzy posed by a boulder half-buried in the beach. She lifted her head and spread her arms before letting forth with song. Her eyes shone, her face alive with the rhythm of the music, the emotion of the lyrics. Kay immediately recognised it as "Besame Mucho." She applauded because it was Fuzzy's song, the one she sang as an encore on hot summer nights for the camp concerts – community gatherings organised by the internees back in the Slocan days. Kay sat down on the ground before her friend, gazing up with misty eyes as she remembered:

Fuzzy rose centre stage. Her voice quivered slightly as she slid to the high notes. Her makeshift gown swayed to the piano, sweeping across the tops of her scuffed high heels. The air of the church hall prickled with the anticipation of a standing ovation.

The lake water lapped softly. The trees behind rustled slightly. It began to rain. Fuzzy stopped and put her hands to her face. Her shoulders shook from sobbing.

Kay quickly moved to her side and gently sat her down on the boulder.

"Fuzzy, what's wrong? Your singing wasn't all that bad." Her attempt to lighten the moment faded in free fall. Her hand shook as she placed it on her friend's shoulder. Tears welled in her own eyes.

"I ... I met someone," she confessed.

"Met someone?"

"In camp. A wonderful, kind man." Fuzzy composed herself and turned to Kay. "I love him."

"Why that's wonderful Fuzzy! I thought something was up from your letter."

"You don't understand! We had to call it off."

Kay's face expressed concern.

"He's going out east and I'm going to Japan." Her hands came up once again.

Kay's mind screamed with defiance. *Stay!* she implored. *Go east. Marry him.* But the words caught in the throat, smothered by impossibilities. Her arms grew heavy and hung by her sides. Her tears flowed over her smooth cheeks. "Damn, Fuzzy, I'm sorry. I'm so sorry. Damn. Damn."

The woods echoed with the sound of falling rain and crying women.

★

Fusae turned on the clockradio and the hotel room filled with a disembodied voice calling on Roy Orbison to sing. She smiled at the gently paced music that broke the silence of the place. It was a functional room, simple, hardly what was called elegant. It would do.

She smoothed her ankle-length skirt as she sat on the hard bed with the polyester cover. One leg placed in front of the other. Proper posture. Her nails were a bit long. *Must cut them or they'll snag on the material at work.*

Every so often she looked at the time. She didn't recognise the song. American. Kind of sad actually.

A muffled knock at the door woke her out of her languor. At her invitation, a stiffly tall bellboy entered, his head bowed to avoid eye contact. The lines of his neat black jacket and pants were sharp and well defined. She motioned him to set the bottle and glasses on the end table. He complied, uttering some perfunctory Japanese before making his exit.

She looked at the clock once again. One o'clock. Midnight April 20th in Canada. Our anniversary. She opened the champagne and filled both glasses. The bubbles danced to the surface before popping. *Cheaper than French but just as sparkling*, she noted. She filled both glasses and raised one.

"Kay," she whispered.

January 10, 1996

Dear Fuzzy,

I'm coming! That's right, I'm coming to Tokyo! I've decided this is the year. How long has it been since I last saw you? 50 years this year? No, it can't be. It goes by so quickly. I'll write with specific dates soon.

Looking forward to seeing you!

Kay

To the day, she thought. The liquid fizzled up to her nose. Fuzzy pulled the glass away quickly and grimaced at the sharp explosions in her nostrils. She thought about Kay: her small face with the red sobbing eyes saying goodbye; her cropped straight hair growing progressively matted by the rain. She had decided to move east. *Had it tough in the beginning but at least she married a good man and had two children. She did all right.*

Fusae closed her eyes and felt the shame well up inside her, congealing in her throat. *Better time of it than I had. Japan was a country bombed out when we came here. Nearly starved to death. We were gaijin. No one wanted us here. No one talked to us, much less helped us. Only me left. Still barely making it.* She rubbed her arm and casually fingered the frayed collar of the rumpled blouse. *Kay must feel embarrassed, by herself in that room ... but it was the right choice ...*

February 15, 1996

Dear Kay,

Please don't come. It would be too much for me to see you again. I wouldn't be able to bear it. You understand.

It has been fifty years. Let's pretend to meet. Rent a hotel room in Toronto on the 19th of April and give me a toast at midnight. I'll do the same. We can meet in our thoughts and you will see me as I was.

Fusae

The Tokyo streets darkened with the rain. The mid-afternoon roar could not be muffled. Contorted neon buzzed as the tide of shoppers and *salarymen* ebbed and flowed. Only she heard Roy Orbison crescendo and descend into a sublime blue silence.

The Moment of Truth

A woman dressed in black waits patiently on her veranda. She is tall, with thin hips and no discernible waist or bosom. Hard to believe she has had three children. But that was long ago, over thirty years since the last was born.

She carries herself with dignity. Her arms are crossed in front of her. Her legs, covered by an understated long skirt, stand pressed together.

A Buick pulls up to the curb in front of her two-storey brick home partially hidden by an exploding lilac. The bush's shock of spring purple gives no hint of the darkness that pools behind it. The house is an anonymous part of a working-class neighbourhood on the edge of town where urban meets suburban. The Victorian-style semi-detached homes in the area were built in the 1920s to accommodate labourers and their families who found prosperity during the construction boom after World War I.

The woman gingerly steps down to the front walk. The new high-heeled shoes pinch at her feet but she doesn't complain.

A young man, dressed in a dark suit, gets out of the car and moves to meet her at the passenger door. He briefly makes eye contact before taking her gloved hand. The Brylcream in his hair catches the shine of the noon sun. His clean, almost sharp features seem cast in cement. He never moves his tightly cut lips, not even to say hello to his mother.

The thud of air pressure and vacuum echoes up and down the street as he slams the car door behind her. He circles the front, opens his door and slides in behind the wheel. A momentary pause before the roar of the engine upsets nearby cats. The car pulls away slowly and drives up toward the bustle of a main street that leads downtown.

Across the street, sixteen-year-old Michael Akamatsu sits alone on his veranda watching Mrs. Fitzgerald waiting on her veranda –

167

two solitary figures separated by more than physical distance. Her black dress stands in sharp contrast to the purple bush. He holds a special interest in her since she can confirm the rumours that have been circulating around the neighbourhood.

As he clicks on his transistor radio, the speaker crackles before pulling in the heavy sounds of CHUM-AM. Sitar strains coat the backbeat as the Top Forty psychedelia begins its interminable run. He jerks the Radio King from his ear and adjusts the volume before pressing it again to his head. He makes a token effort to push back his long dark hair, which is forever getting in his way. The unruly, unstyled mop is his front line of defiance.

When the blue Buick with a hint of back fins slowly drives up to the front of her house, Michael smiles. His full lips stretch thin and expose a straight set of teeth. He sees the funeral flag on the antennae. "So it's true," he whispers. "Old Fitz is dead."

The car manoeuvres up the street. Michael leans back to lie on the rough mat on his veranda. He squints in the sunlight that is fractured by a ceiling of green maple leaves held up by the mature trees that line his street – the street where he had faced the moment of truth and lost everything.

★

The Beatles sang their songs through their smiles on the Ed Sullivan Show. Sunday night and with every shake of hair and gyration of hips, the audience of mainly prepubescent girls screamed their enjoyment for the television cameras.

Twelve-year-old Michael slid back from the ten-inch screen, the seat of his heavy corduroy pants rasping along the linoleum. His mother chortled, her jowls jiggling, her thick thighs vibrating in sympathy.

"*Maaa*, what crazy music!" she exclaimed in Japanese. "I can't believe it." She laughed out loud at the shot of a sobbing girl mouthing an idol's name.

"Mama, you're kichigai too!" Michael's father said, startled by the outburst. Lying on the couch, he stroked the stubble on his prominent chin and contemplated the scene with a bemused expression.

"Hakujin do funny things, don't they?" Mrs. Akamatsu declared.

Michael looked back and forth from his parents to the television screen. "Boy, they *are* nuts!" he blurted in agreement. He turned again, his eyes widening to take in as much as he could. He became aware of the bristles of his brush-cut hair. His feet tapped with the rhythm of the music. The refrain swirled in his head.

In his parents' upstairs bedroom later that evening, Michael listened from the master bed to the faint muttering of prayer his mother performed in front of the *hotokesama*. He had left his father slumped in his easy chair in the living room, dozing in front of the television set. Michael never disturbed either of his parents. A great gulf of silence and experience lay between them. Their rudimentary knowledge of English and the imperatives of Japanese culture governing children divided them. He knew what they were saying for the most part and he did try to connect. But never in Japanese. Every night he gazed at the family altar visible to the left of his mother's soft sloping back, at the black and white photographs framed to preserve the memory of dead relatives, strangers to him but loved ones to her.

He did remember standing in front of their graves in Japan about six years ago. His parents had decided to take him on a trip to discover his heritage. His apprehension was fanned by his friends.

"Hey Mike, you gotta go and give them Japs what for."

"Yeah, show 'em what Canadians are made of!"

Ken Fleming, Frank Wayne and Mike Akamatsu made up a trio of pals who lived close to one another and were of the same age. Michael spent a great deal of time at his friends' houses, but, oddly, he never invited them into his home even though they often gathered on his front porch. Ken's parents were the rich ones on the street, a half-block down. Mr. Fleming, grey and suffering from premature curvature of the spine, was a bank manager and drove a

luxury-model Chevrolet. Mrs. Fleming, a heavyset matron from
the British Isles, took it upon herself to set the tone for the neighbourhood. Accordingly, she was tolerant of Michael to a point. She
once told neighbours he should play with kids of "his own kind
down in Chinatown".

"You spend too much time here," she said to him.

Frank's father, a Canadian Army war veteran, always wore his
beret and often sat on the veranda steps, working on beer and
memory.

"Mike-*san*," he growled, "you stay away from my kids. We did-
n't finish the job as far as I'm concerned."

Michael didn't quite know what he meant by that, but he was
afraid of that gaunt face with the red, cracked eyes and bone-dry
hands, and the sour smell of him.

"Sure Mike, you're a Canadian!" said Frank, surreptitiously
winking at Ken. "You gotta make them Nips pay!"

Ken stepped forward. "Mike, make us proud of you."

Michael was surprised by the encouragement of his friends, yet
he liked the swell of nationalism in his chest. "Yeah, I'll get them
Japs," he said nervously, his eyes darting side to side.

The incense burned steadily and its smoke clung to the ground,
the stone grave markers in the rural Japanese cemetery acting like
anchors. The summer air was still and heavy with humidity. The
bonsan chanted a steady stream of Sanskrit verse while the crowd of
Akamatsu relatives quietly observed the ritual.

Michael found Japan a completely foreign experience. No
"Frosted Flakes" in the morning – only fish and rice. No running
water, no indoor washrooms. The milk tasted "funny". And no
one spoke English, making him strain to understand every conversation.

At the cemetery, he met all his relatives, living and dead, before
paying respect to the ancestors. Feeling shy and not wishing to talk
to anyone, he stood by his mother solemnly. With the drone of the
minister in the background and the sweet, cloying smell of the in-

cense dulling his senses, he turned away and looked to the distance. Above the horizon, black smoke poured from a smokestack atop an anonymous building.

"Mama, what's that?" he asked, pointing to the billowing clouds.

"Mai-ko, shii!"

"Mama … mama," he persisted.

She relented and looked up. "Oh, that's where they get rid of dead horses."

"Get rid of horses? How?"

"They burn them up."

They burn them up. The sentence gave Michael pause. He then took notice of all the grave stones around him. Most bore his last name. An aunt who had overheard the conversation teased him about his mother's fate. "Your okāsan will be burned up too when the time comes." Dread suddenly filled his rapidly mounting thoughts. Michael burst into tears and reached for his mother's arms, crying "No! No!" at the same time.

The crowd glared at him in disdain, but the *bonsan* continued undisturbed.

After the ceremony, Michael was assigned to his young cousins' care. As the group of three stood on the gravel road outside the slumping homestead of wooden walls and bamboo roof, he knew they weren't exactly thrilled to be with the crying boy. Tatsuo, the lean and older one, laughed while he spoke to his brother Satomi, chubby and younger. "Look at this *gaijin*! He's like all Americans, stupid looking!" he said in a mocking Japanese.

"You shut up," warned Michael, resorting to English. "I'll show you …" He remembered his friends' encouragement as he pulled back a fist and let go.

Tatsuo shifted slightly, caught the fist in the crook of his arm, twisted and hurled his assailant over his shoulder. Michael hit the ground with arm and knees extended. The thud and scrape shocked him. Cloth tore, skin split. The flush of pain blocked all efforts to understand what had just happened.

The two brother-cousins laughed as they ran down the road to-

ward the village. Michael sat up, his tears stinging the bleeding
knee that had popped through his pants. He remained in the road a
long time nursing his wounds and contemplating the merits of being a Canadian.

Shortly after the incident, Michael began having a recurring
dream.

> *He is standing alone in a field. At least, he feels alone. Men are*
> *working behind him but he can't see them. Digging, he guesses.*
> *Anxiety like a current of electricity suddenly rips through his*
> *body and he wakes up sweating.*

The dream followed him home to Canada. Throughout his
childhood and early adolescence, Michael eyed his parents with
uneasiness. He imagined each withering away, falling to the
ground in a lifeless heap. Even as his mother laughed with friends
over a meal of *chow mein* take-out or as his father figured out his
strategy for the Japanese Credit Union meeting, his heart would
beat faster, his breathing would quicken. He panicked at the
thought of death.

"Mai-ko, what's wrong with you?"

The scream in his head subsided and he answered with silence.
Fear evaporated, leaving an inexplicable residue of guilt.

★

"Did you see those guys last night?"

"They were cool."

"Yeah, I love that song. "'I Wanna' ... 'I Wanna' ...""

""I Wanna Hold Your Hand,' dummy."

School was abuzz with the excitement of the new. The girls
gushed over the relative "cuteness" of the band members. The boys
indulged in vicarious fantasy. Frank, Ken and Mike carried their
enthusiasm back home to Mike's veranda. They stood together
steaming the cold winter air with their conversation.

"We should form a group," Ken proposed.

Frank curled his lip. "And do what?"

"Play."

"But none of us can play instruments," Michael reminded.

Ken responded quickly. "So we'll fake it."

"What?"

"Listen, I got their album. We'll play it and we'll play along to them." The two seemed sceptical. "I've got two guitars. Frank, you can rig something for drums."

"I guess I could use boxes. My parents save all kinds."

Ken continued, "We'll give a concert in my basement. You know, call all the kids in the neighbourhood."

They envisioned the black and white hysteria of the night before. Anticipation grew.

"Hey, what'll we call ourselves?"

Ken turned and declared, "The Box Men."

"*Mai-ko!*" A voice from inside the house. "*Gohan!*" The door opened. Mrs. Akamatsu's large form filled the doorway.

"Gotta go, guys."

"Wait, Mike. Can we practise at your place tonight?" asked Ken.

"I don't know," he said shaking his head. Ken stepped towards Mike's mother.

"Mrs. Akamatsu, can we come over tonight?"

She lowered her eyes, her face flushed as she turned away. "*Mai-ko, hayaku!*"

Mike moved to the door. "I gotta go. It's supper. I can't practise tonight. Maybe tomorrow. Okay?" He followed his mother inside.

Two weeks later The Box Men made their debut. Word had gotten out quickly and every kid in the neighbourhood knew where to be Saturday night.

Ken was enterprising and charged a ten-cent entrance fee. His father approved of his son's initiative even though Mrs. Fleming worried about the kind of children that filled their newly finished basement.

The rec room was dark with the pungent smell of moth-balls and fresh plaster. Candles melted onto plastic skulls flickered in corners. By eight o'clock, the room bustled with an audience unsure of what to expect.

An unseen hand switched on red and blue Christmas spotlights to reveal an arrangement of four cardboard boxes of varying sizes in front of the entrance to the furnace room. Two broken hockey sticks with paper cups glued to one end stood in boxes in front. A portable record player sat beside the "drums".

A smatter of applause raced through the crowd and camphor as the three Box Men came out of the furnace room. They were dressed in similar red shirts and white pants. One sat behind the boxes with two well-used drum sticks. The other two stood in front of the "mikes" with worn nylon-string guitars, refugees from the misbegotten guitar lessons of older siblings. Ken was obviously the leader. His height, sandy blond hair, copious freckles, and clear blue eyes placed him high on the "cuteness" scale for the girls in the audience. Frank, with his dark complexion, thin body and intense eyes gave off an aura of danger, of juvenile delinquency. Mike seemed the friendliest with his smile and stocky build. He was the perennial sidekick.

The scratchy pop of audio needle to record surface signalled the beginning of the concert. The surge of music set the musicians in motion. They shook, gyrated and screamed in a pantomime of their heroes. The girls squealed. The boys clapped in time to the beat. People started to dance. By the third song, the room was thick with excitement.

Side one ended and an awkward silence settled in. Everyone squinted as the lights switched on abruptly.

"Boys and girls!" called a familiar voice. "Come upstairs to the kitchen. I've got refreshments for you all." Mrs. Fleming beckoned from the foot of the basement stairs.

The Box Men followed the crowd of about twenty to the roomy kitchen where milk and cookies awaited them. Mrs. Fleming motioned the trio of musicians through the adjoining dining room to the front sitting room.

"Son, that was a good performance," said Mr. Fleming, a craggy, slightly bent man in a business suit sitting on the large couch that dominated the room.

"You saw?"

"We all did," he said gesturing to his friends, the Fitzgeralds, who lived up the street. "We came down when the, um, music started."

Mrs. Grace Fitzgerald perched on the edge of an imitation Queen Anne chair, Mrs. Fleming's pride and joy. Mrs. Fitzgerald's greying hair was kept curly and short by her downtown stylist. Her clothes were demure but smart in design. She smiled in agreement, waiting for her husband to do the talking.

Detective John Fitzgerald shot the boys a grin from his slumped position within a too-comfortable armchair. The body cut in half, his six-foot height was imperceptible. The short moustache, the tightly cropped hair, the broad forehead, the muscular build gave him the air of authority needed to be a policeman. At the same time, his jovial air and easy manner afforded him the opportunity to rough-house with the local kids. "Fitz" took every chance to pick up a hockey stick and join the kids in the street to take a few slapshots at a nervous goalie. He enjoyed wrestling with some, tossing water balloons at others, and joking with most. All the rough-housing reminded him of his three sons when they were young and playing in the street during the great days before World War II, before he left with the army for the South Pacific.

"You guys did all right with your *yeah, yeah, yeahs!*" Fitz laughed. "Ken, come here for a sec."

At that moment, Mrs. Fleming excused herself to supervise the children in the kitchen. Frank and Mike moved to the middle room to help themselves to the sandwiches Mrs. Fleming had arranged for her adult guests. They remained within earshot.

Mike caught snatches of the conversation. "Why do you need that Japanese ... brings you down ... nobody wants to see ..." The memory of a recent road hockey game came to mind as he turned away from Fitz and Ken.

★

Fitz takes command of the tennis ball with his stick. He looks for Frank, passes it to him. He turns and sees Mike watching the play develop. Fitz steps sideways and knocks him to the ground. He sniggers at the crumpled boy as he retrieves the ball–puck, takes aim and fires a high shot at Ken in goal. Ken's glove sweeps up automatically and catches the missile.

Fitz slaps the startled goalie on the back, congratulating him. He grabs Frank around the shoulders at the same time. The other neighbourhood players mill about the trio.

"Good play, guys. Well, I gotta go. The Missus wants me in for dinner. I'll see you later."

Mike looks up from his prone position. Fitz lumbers up his walk, his jacket casually tossed over his shoulder, his hand wiping the sweat off his forehead with a handkerchief. The boy hears the mocking laughter of his cousins in Japan.

★

Mike and his fellow Box Men resumed with side two. The temperature and excitement of the room built faster this time as if everyone knew the evening would soon be over. Ken and Mike, the two front men, began shouting the lyrics as Frank cranked up the record player as loud as it would go. The crowd jumped up and jerked and twisted in a frenzied dance.

The novelty wore off by spring. Life for the boys returned to normal. Fitz continued to join the daily street games after work. He joked with Ken, terrorised him with high-velocity slapshots, and generally clowned with the others. Mike moved to the fringe of the game to avoid catching Fitz's attention. When the boys weren't scuffling up and down the street, they played their favourite weekend game – Guns. Influenced by television and the weekly features at the Eastwood Movie Theatre, they saw themselves as William

Holden landing on the beaches of Normandy or John Wayne climbing the hills of Iwo Jima.

The local laneway, across from the Fleming house, ran from the street and met a large sandlot before curving away to run behind the houses. "The Dump", a junkyard paradise of rusting cars, exposed bedsprings and worn-out appliances, was the ideal playground for boys with vivid imaginations. The sand dunes, jutting rocks and sloping cliffs that climbed to the railway tracks resembled the landscape of movies with titles like *Battle Cry!* and *From Hell to Eternity.*

The D.W. Tomlinson Company owned the vacant land. Tomlinson, a grocer, had taken advantage of the prosperity of the 1950s and built several storage warehouses across the lane from the houses. The dump was land gone fallow, intended for later expansion.

The three boys thought of it as their territory. Armed with wooden sticks or plastic guns, they defended the land against intruders and pretenders.

"Frank, who's that?" Ken asked.

"Where?"

"Up on top."

Five figures combed the terrain like ants on an ant hill.

"Looks like kids from across the tracks."

"C'mon."

Mike felt himself pulled along. "Where?"

"To get rid of those guys!" Ken yelled.

As the three scaled the heights, they taunted the enemy. "Hey you creeps, get outta here." "Who do you think you are?" "We're gonna get you guys!" Frank raised his imitation carbine and pulled the trigger. The caps sparked and the noise echoed.

A strange echo ricocheted. The sand near Frank's feet danced. A second later, Frank let out a cry, his gun flying down the incline. He fell to the dirt, his hands covering his face.

The tallest of the gang holding the high ground lowered his rifle and let out a whoop. The others picked up rocks and hurled them down upon their assailants.

Mike could see the smirk beneath the wire-rimmed glasses of the leader. He jerked Frank's hands away from his face and found his cheek bleeding. Ken soon reached them and hustled them down the precipice, rocks landing all around them.

Where the laneway joined the street, Ken decided that Frank had been hit by a BB from an air rifle. Mike wiped his dirt-smudged face before noticing the blood on his hand. Wounded by a rock.

A chorus of distant catcalls stabbed deeper into wounds and hearts.

The heat shimmered above the fire. Ashes flaked off the greying wood and floated mid-air, caught in the updraft. Buried in the nest of kindling and combustion were six potatoes covered with aluminium foil. They looked like the eggs of a story book phoenix.

Two of the boys crouched by the fire, poking the potatoes from time to time. Ken stood to "keep a lookout". He trained his new Winchester BB rifle on the cliffs of the dump.

"Will you sit down!" ordered Frank. His face seemed drawn, all lines converging on the slight scar on his cheek. "It's been two weeks and we ain't seen those guys."

"Yeah but they're there," Ken answered self-consciously.

"So what?"

"So we'll be ready for them next time."

Next time? Mike shuddered at the prospect.

The potatoes were hot but crunchy. Mike didn't mind. He enjoyed the apple texture. His mother made them too soft on the rare occasion he had potatoes rather than rice for dinner.

The boys lay back on the ground after their meal and relaxed their guard.

Something occurred to Mike. "Ken, you ever think about your parents?"

"Yeah sure, all the time, especially around allowance time," he said laughing as he gave his rifle a pat.

"No, I mean seriously. You ever think about them croaking?"

"You mean dying? What're you talking about? Yours dying soon?"

"No ... no, I mean it'd be awful if they did. I keep trying to talk to them about stuff but I can't get through to them ... them being Japanese and all."

Ken jerked his head up and shushed Mike at the same time. He heard someone approaching. In the distance, he saw Fitz walking up the laneway from the street. "Hey, hey, get your guns. I got an idea."

The other two crawled over to Ken.

"That's just Fitz," Frank said.

"Yeah, let's scare him."

"What?" asked the other two.

"C'mon, it'll be fun," Ken called as he crept quickly to where the laneway met the sand, and hid among garbage cans destined for the Dump. Behind him, Mike and Frank took up positions in nearby bushes. Fitz continued to walk up the lane on his way to his garage, unaware of any ambush.

At the crucial moment, all three jumped from their hiding places, their cap pistols and BB rifle blazing. Fitz reared straight up and staggered in surprise. He recovered quickly.

In one swift motion, he grabbed Mike, the closest to him, by the back of the shirt and pulled out his service revolver. He roughly placed the barrel right between the boy's eyes.

"So you think you got the drop on ol' Fitz," he spat, his voice quivering with the adrenaline.

Time stood suspended. Mike's mind traced the circle of the barrel mouth. Electricity shot down his legs as if his self were draining from him. Death breathed in his face.

"You little Jap. I oughta pull the trigger ..." He pushed the boy to the ground. Still aiming the revolver, he growled with contempt, "I oughta, for the boys I left behind. God damn it, I oughta." Tears blinded him. He lowered the weapon and slouched his way up the back alley.

No one said a thing. No one could. When Ken and Frank saw Fitz pull his revolver, invisible hands grabbed their throats in a choke-hold. Their hollow legs became weighed down with cement, their throats desert dry. Even as Fitz moved away, they couldn't move. Frank's left hand shook slightly.

Mike felt the sharp edges of the gravel. He scraped the ground with his hands. The charcoal roughness turned red with his blood.

The boy stood before his mother shivering, a mass of mixed emotions. He felt pulverised and scattered, like dust dancing in light. In his mind, he could still hear his friends calling after him as he ran up the street, away from them. The raised eyebrows, the pained look in his mother's eyes spoke of her dismay at the condition of his clothes and the torn skin of his palms.

"Where have you been?" Mrs. Akamatsu barked. "Look at those dungarees. Do you know how much these things cost?"

As his mother spanked his bottom in an effort to punish him and to clean the fabric at the same time, Mike thought about telling her. He even saw himself breaking down and crying in her comforting arms.

He then imagined his mother wilting before Fitz's dismissive glare, contemptuous of her quaking English. In the rain of scolding Japanese words, he kept his mouth shut and stood silently, a burning ring pressing between his eyes.

★

At the bottom of the veranda steps, Mrs. Grace Fitzgerald brushes lint from her black dress before walking down the path to the car. Mike can see the dams of mascara lines beneath the eyes maintaining her decorum, but it is the eyes, red from tears and rubbing hands, that speak of her true state.

She shouldn't feel so bad, he thinks. Not for him. He deserved that heart attack.

The car gone, insouciant winds remain. Mike sits up and casts his mind back. The Beatles. The screaming girls. The first and last performance of The Box Men. He swallows at what has come to be. If he passes Ken or Frank in the street, their eyes avert, their mouths remain mute. There is a pane of glass between him and them. After the incident, he has become a stranger to them; they are kept away by his anger.

Mike hasn't spent any time in the Dump in four years. Neither has he picked up a hockey stick. He likes to think he no longer cares about his parents; he considers them to be foreigners.

"Mai-ko, where are you going? Will you be home for gohan?" his mother asks on almost a daily basis.

His temper flares but he does not answer.

Mike stays up very late most nights and goes to sleep only when exhausted in an effort to avoid a new recurring dream.

> *The grave, freshly dug, with Fitz's headstone. He stands over it, his awkward body shaking. A cold wind brushes against his face. Phlegm chokes his throat. He spits on the dirt and grinds the wetness into the earth. He looks down discovering it's his parents' grave.*

Mai-ko always wakes with a start, his face awash with tears.

Message in a Bottle

ANOTHER HOME: *1959 Japan*

Blue whales wave goodbye
among Fukui whitecaps.

Winter clouds unfurl
          home again
potted flowers
in the
          sewing room

His breathing was erratic, so desperate at times I thought his lungs would burst. His long, drawn face, his dried-out limbs, his vacant eyes frightened me. The crisp white sheets of the hospital bed cloaked the phlegm and bile of Father's illness from public view. I backed out of the semi-private room stunned and alone, bumping into furniture and equipment, apologising incoherently to inanimate objects.

In the echoing corridor, painted green and scoured with alcohol, I heard voices spinning about me. The voices of professionals, medical and religious: *"I doubt he has much longer. Pneumonia acts quickly. Maybe today, probably tomorrow. I'm sorry Mr. Watada ... Better be prepared to let him go. I'm ready when you need me ... Have you thought about the funeral?"*

I moved away from everyone and into the maze of hospital corridors looking for an exit. I fought back the tears in an effort to deny the obvious and to avert the inevitable.

The telephone screamed in the darkness. Two a.m. My eyes barely broke the bonds of sleep as my hand groped towards the receiver. The heavy air of the bedroom pressed against my temples. My T-shirt stuck to my chest.

A dull, passionless voice called from the bottom of a dank pit. "Mr. Wy-nata?" The mispronunciation meant it wasn't anyone I knew. "Mr. Wy-nata, your father passed away about a half-hour ago. I'm sorry." The words hit like a soft rain; meaning lingered on the surface before seeping in slowly.

All I could muster was an inappropriate, choking "Thank you." I hung up. My back cracked as I pulled myself up to a seated position. When I turned on the lamp, I sheltered my eyes from the flood of light which offered little comfort in my darkness. The room's humidity felt leaden, and I began to shudder beneath the weight.

185

*You were a good father, but I was an angry, selfish son. "No
fight with mama," you begged me when I fought against the
guilt okāsan placed on me over you. I just couldn't forgive you
for what you had become. Your stiff legs scraped up the stairs one
by one as if hauled by some invisible winch. At the top landing,
you saw me, my youth smouldering. You stood motionless,
paralysed by old age and Parkinson's. You shook; your face
drained of expression. You couldn't hit me, scold me or even reason with me. The tactics of parenthood had fallen from you like
leaves from a tree in decline. I called you "fool". You burst into
tears. Slowly, I put my arm around you. Only one. I could
manage only one.*

I wiped away the tears on my cheek and drifted to my childhood, the time of fathers. Back then, he had thick, muscular arms,
and he towered above me, strong, rugged and clear eyed. My father
had been a lumberjack, climbing the giant evergreens of British
Columbia. During gin games at our house in Toronto, his friends
often told me of his exploits as a highrigger on Vancouver Island.

★

"You don't know your otōsan too good, do you?" growled the
grizzled one with a concave face and alcoholic's nose.

I looked away from the horrible face and sought my mother's
dress to hide behind. The rush of the harsh Japanese words scared
me, an eight-year-old boy. I turned away from meaning.

"Well, he was a good worker in the old days. Best highrigger I
ever saw. From six in the morning to quitting time, he worked. I
never seen him tire. Hey bōshin, you never tired, eh?"

"Rik-san, you're drunk. Stop scaring my son," Father admonished as he sat back to enjoy the moment. "He can't understand
Japanese."

Rik-*san* ignored him and turned to me again. "He once saved
my life, bōzu. Pulled me out of the way of a donkey winch. The
wire snapped and would've cut me in half!"

As a child, I could talk to my father in "baby" Japanese. I lost any potential of conversing with him fully with Saturday morning television. Cartoon characters made more sense. He made his friends laugh heartily into the night when he felt free to speak his native tongue, but he could communicate with his second son only through a combination of sign language, primary Japanese phrases and broken English. Nonetheless, it was in this haphazard manner that I learned about his arrival in Vancouver.

★

As a second son, Matsujiro Watada, my father, stood to inherit nothing from the family farm in Fukui-*ken*, Japan. His father, Ginaburo Watada, a practical man with a paradoxically adventurous spirit, offered to take his son to Canada. Grandfather had been to the great foreign land of white devils and plentiful work several times during his lifetime. He assured his son that he would feel right at home in Vancouver's Little Tokyo. Matsujiro agreed, his fourteen-year-old heart pounding for high adventure.

Vancouver's East End bustled with the activity of enterprising immigrants. Parallel streets, East Hastings and Powell, cut through the intersections of Main, Dunlevy and Jackson to hem the Japanese into the area known as Little Tokyo. Stores marketed Japanese foodstuffs; churches offered spiritual comfort; bars (called "hotels") sold secular comfort; and rooming-houses rented a place to sleep. Little Tokyo was considered a piece of home but was in reality a comfortable ghetto. So it was in 1920, when Father and Grandfather, upon arriving, rented space in Amitani's Rooming House at Powell and Jackson.

Matsujiro took the first few days to wander through the area, familiarising himself with what was available. At some point he came across the Georgia Cafe, a four-stool ma-and-pa operation on the outskirts of Little Tokyo. Father sat down, curious for a first taste of *yōshoku*. His confidence faltered when the cook, a multiple-chinned white man with a gruff voice, confronted him in English. "What'll it be, Mac?"

Matsujiro didn't understand a word. He stared as if he were deaf. The cook wiped his nose on his sleeve as he slid his customer a menu.

Matsujiro shifted his gaze from his antagonist to the menu and back again. Meaning finally dawned on him. He opened the menu to a wall of hieroglyphics spreading before him.

"Well?" said the owner in an impatient tone.

In a panic, Father pointed to an item.

"Sausage and eggs? Okay buddy, you got it."

The man shrugged as he broke a couple of eggs. Matsujiro smiled secretly. *E-gu, sa ... sa ...* He struggled to form the words. He soon gave up, deciding instead just to point. Two weeks later, he stopped going to the Georgia Cafe, sick of the taste of sausage and eggs three meals a day.

Ginaburo's contacts in the Japanese lumber business soon turned up a job for his son. Matsujiro became a trainee labourer for the Toyama Sawmill on False Creek. His wage was twenty-five cents an hour for a ten-hour day, six days a week. Meagre, but enough to survive.

After two weeks, Ginaburo took his son up to their one-room second-floor flat. They sat facing each other on the bed with its broken back. Grandfather hesitated before speaking. He bowed his head and brought up his hand to rub his eyes.

"Otōsan, what's wrong?" Matsujiro asked innocently.

"Nothing, Mat-chan," he replied as he looked up and smiled broadly. "It's just that I have to go back to Japan."

His son smiled in return. "When are we going?"

"No. I'm going. You can't come with me," he said slowly. "You are staying. You have no future in Japan." Matsujiro's face was still immature, but his body was strong and tall. Ginaburo must have thought my father would be all right.

Grandfather explained he had responsibilities at home with Matsujiro's mother, grandfather, and brothers and sisters. It was time to go.

In a few weeks the ship set sail for the distant ports of Yoko-hama, Singapore and Hong Kong.

★

"I cry when I come Canada," you said to me just a month ago. "Homesick,. you know." I didn't know how to react. After all, you'd never confessed such intimate feelings before. We never talked about feelings at all. Never about problems, goals, life. We couldn't. The language barrier. But maybe you knew this was our last time together and maybe, for some reason, you wanted me to know about your childhood. You and mom took me to Japan in 1959 when I was eight. The pictures of that trip are somewhere around the house. I remember the last photo-graph was of a pot of flowers in Mom's sewing room. You had written underneath it, "Home at last, flowers."

Home was where he came at five o'clock, weary from his floor-grinder's job on a construction site somewhere in the boom-ing metropolis of Toronto in the early 1960s. He was always cov-ered with cement dust. He ruled with a strict hand, but often the hand was gentle and giving.

On a particularly hot summer day when the asphalt streets steamed and melted in the heat shimmer, Father arrived at his usual time. That day, however, he walked through the front door calling my name. As I ran towards him, he held out a molten ice-cream cone, rivulets of cream flowing down his arm. I hugged him and came away with his imprint on my clothes and skin.

★

The morning after Father's death, I phoned my late mother's youngest sister, Aunt Betty. She took the news with a sense of the inevitable. "I suppose it was to be expected," she sighed. I could al-most see her mouth too wide for her narrow, diamond face. "Don't worry, dear, your aunt will take care of things."

She was as good as her word during the days that followed. She arranged for the funeral home, the visitations, the funeral itself, the interment, the Buddhist seventh-day observance, and the collection and answering of *kōden*. She even took care of my out-of-town brother and his family. As she ordered about the hired and the related, her tall, lean figure seemed frail and imposing at the same time. The activity was a great comfort to me. All I had to do was to attend.

The seventh-day observance took place in my house, a semi-detached two-storey brick in Toronto's East End. It had been my parents' home and little had changed. The ceiling was water stained. I vowed I would replace the roof given the time and money. The wallpaper, a faded green with a faint design of swirls, was bubbling and peeling off. The floors were aging, the hardwood stained and chipped.

Everyone stood in the living room waiting for the minister. Aunt Betty banged about in the kitchen with other women volunteered from the ranks of the relatives. I stood reminiscing with male cousins.

"Dad had a private joke about me for years."

The cousins broke into grins.

"When he wanted me, he called me *Ketsu-no ana!*"

The cousins' faces questioned the unfamiliar.

"He did this for years, until one day, I asked him what that meant. He smiled at me and said, 'asshole'! I couldn't believe it. 'All these years, you've been calling me Asshole?' *'Well, you always came!'* was all he said to me."

The rituals and social obligations buzzed by quickly. It seemed like the very next moment all activity stopped. I faced a dark, still and silent house. In my solitude, I looked for his presence if not in body then in some artifact from his past. Mementoes spewed out from cupboards and stiff drawers: broken pocket watches; souvenir buttons; photographs of 19th-century relatives; photos of contemporary ones in Japan; a 1940s postcard collection from Moose Jaw,

Saskatchewan; a set of four *daruma*, each with both eyes filled; and weather-beaten letters. Hundreds of letters, dozens of journals written in Japanese by his elegant hand. But all lay dormant, unintelligible. I was sure there were countless stories before me. I just couldn't decipher them.

With letters and notebooks piled high, I thought about a translator. But I suspected most of the writing consisted of scripture copied by my father as part of his morning ritual. The translator would have to be extremely familiar with Father's religion (a strange mixture of Christianity, Buddhism, and several other randomly picked philosophies) to weed out the anecdotal gems.

As I gazed at the mountain of material, I realised how little I knew of my father's private thoughts, his concerns, his beliefs. I thumbed the documents aimlessly until, unexpectedly, I came across a letter in English, tattered, brown and fragile. The frayed envelope was postmarked *Navy Department, Washington D.C., December 6, 1921.* Inside was a letter from an L.R. Steiguer, Captain, U.S. Navy, Hydrographer, addressed to *Mr. Shinboye Watami, Kiyama Hitomura, Mikatagun, Fukuiken, Japan.* Shinboye Watami? Was this a distant relative of mine? The name had to be misspelled. Watami was Watada, for sure. The address certainly seemed familiar from all the letters to home my parents had written. But why had a Navy hydrographer written to my relatives in Japan? The letter read simply:

> *Sir:*
>
> There is enclosed herewith a letter thrown overboard at sea, April 15, 1920, and addressed to you. This letter was picked up by a native, near Nickolski Village, Umnak Island, Alaska, in September, 1921.

Further scrounging produced the original letter found by that native. I was elated. The writing was faded, nearly obliterated; the paper dry and cracked at the corners. I also didn't know the circumstances surrounding its existence, but at last I had something that definitely contained my father's own words. The naval officer's message was a good starting point.

I hastily called Aunt Betty. Her smoker's voice was comforting in its low growl. She gradually recalled the story of the letter.

"When your father came over the first time on the ... on the ..." She groped for the name. "The *Manila Maru*, yeah that's it ... on the *Manila Maru* with his father, he wrote that letter to his grandfather, your great-grandfather, back in Japan. The Japanese back then always wrote to the head of the household. None of this personal stuff to sisters or mothers or cousins.

"Anyhow, he never had a chance to mail the letter until he got to Vancouver. Even then he forgot all about it."

"So he didn't throw it off the *Manila Maru*?"

"That's what he told me."

Umnak Island is part of the Fox Islands, the beginning set of the Aleutian chain and the first land mass separated from the Alaska Peninsula. Nickolski Village is a settlement on the southwestern tip of that island. According to a postscript in the U.S. Navy letter, the Kuroshio or Black Current off the Canadian west coast must have carried the bottle up the coast to where the Aleut found it. He immediately took it to an American hydrographic survey team stationed on Unalaska, the adjacent island in the chain. An enterprising, if slightly paranoid, Donald H. Stevenson subsequently mailed the letter to Washington for translation. Given the times and his station in life, Stevenson probably thought it to be a clever device for sending coded secrets by coastline spies. After it cleared investigation by Naval Intelligence in D.C., Captain Steiguer, as a representative of the department which had taken custody of the bottle, mailed the letter with an explanatory note to Japan. My father retrieved it in 1930, his first trip home since coming to Canada; he braved the seas again to marry my mother.

That evening, I contacted two friends to translate. Shinobu and Lucy Tanaka, a dynamic and unusual couple, immigrated to Canada several years ago to give their children a North American education. Shinobu, with his beard and radical outlook, had felt unsuited to the provincialism of Japan. His wife Lucy, with her Saskatchewan-nurtured skin and Anglican upbringing, had felt a nostalgia for Canada even though she had been in Japan since she was six. In about two hours, they had translated the letter. What emerged was not earth shattering, but I did hear my father speak as a young teenager.

April 15, 1920

Hello to the household:

Is everyone in the Watada family the same? Working as usual? I am safely crossing the ocean without running into any major storms. I am safe. Don't worry. Since I left, the waves were big for two to three days. All the women were seasick. But I was fine and had a good time. I've made a lot of friends. And I'm having a good time on the boat.

My mother, my older brother and my older sister and so on, not a day goes by that I fail to think of them. Tell them not to worry about me. These days I'm sure that you must be very busy and tired out [exhausted].

In every direction, I see nothing but sea, and when I look at the sky, I see nothing but clouds. At this busiest time for farmers, I'm just spending money, eating, sleeping and playing so it feels wasteful [I feel guilty]. At last [distorted] has come.

I would like to write more, but I'll finish here. It will get hotter and hotter so please everyone take care.

From the ship,
Watada

p.s.   To whoever finds this, I would appreciate it if you would send this to Watada, Shinbei; Kiyama Hito-mura; Mikata-gun; Fukui-ken; Japan.

Although addressed to "the household", the letter was meant for his grandfather, as evidenced by the very formal style of writing. Even with his limited education (eighth grade at the most) and age, Father was quite skilled at expressing himself.

I found it curious that he never said in the letter that he was homesick, as he had confessed to me just before his death. In fact,

Matsujiro sounded like he was on a great adventure. He struck up friendships, weathered the storms, ate copiously and played to his heart's content. The ocean and clouds seemed as endless as his life. He felt a certain amount of guilt, but those feelings soon disappeared, I was sure, when he saw the green mountains rising above Vancouver Harbour ahead of him. He knew at that moment the power of youth, the expanse of life ahead of him and the riches to be fought for and won. I could see him on the beach throwing the message in the bottle into the flow of the Kuroshio. It carried all his hopes, his aspirations, the dreams of youth.

Aunt Betty lived by herself below Queen Street in the East End. She and her husband moved to Toronto from British Columbia after the war. Her English was quite good, thanks to night school and a burning desire to better herself. Shortly after settling in the poor working-class neighbourhood, she told her husband she wanted to live in a bungalow in either of the suburbs of East York or Scarborough. That was a mark of genuine prosperity. The ambition never came to fruition. Her husband died of lung cancer in the '60s, the same disease that took my mother, her sister, in the late 1980s, three years before Father. She became resigned to living out her life beside the Canada Metal Plant in Toronto's industrial area. My mother's death drew us closer together since she had no children.

As I knocked on her door, I noticed how deteriorated the veranda seemed. The paint peeled and the floor sagged in the middle.

"Terry! Come in, come in," she greeted as she gestured inside.

The narrow hallway to the inside was dark and musty. Even the overhead lamp cast only a dull light. A doorless opening in the corridor led to a sitting room with overstuffed couches, a heavy coffee table and sepia photographs on the walls. I sank into the seat she offered as she disappeared into the kitchen. "Aunt Betty, could you tell me a bit more about Dad?"

"Well, I don't know all that much," she said, preparing green tea and arranging a tray of cookies. An obvious understatement.

Her thin arms reminded me of tree limbs in winter, bare and fragile against a stiff Arctic wind.

She poured the tea. "What do you want to know?" The cookies were stale.

I read the letter to her, and she told me again about the circumstances surrounding it.

"Why didn't Dad mention his father on the boat with him?" I asked.

She thought a moment and guessed, "Well, he probably knew your grandfather would be writing home himself, so why bother?"

"Why not mention him, just as a courtesy?"

"I don't know!" she exclaimed. "You're asking me to read your father's thoughts, how many years ago?"

"I'm sorry, Aunt Betty," I responded contritely. "Maybe you can answer this one. I thought he was homesick when he came to Canada."

"Told me he was."

"Doesn't sound like it in the letter."

"Of course not. He was excited, being on a boat trip with his dad for the first time and all," she explained. "It was only after he was left to go it alone, when his father left for Japan. That's when he must've got really homesick and decided on the message in a bottle. You know, kid stuff." She paused a moment. "My guess is he kinda felt like that bottle."

"What do you mean?"

"Well, he knew there wasn't much chance of him ever going back to Japan, and he knew that throwing the bottle into the ocean was probably a useless thing. But at least there was a chance his words would get back home."

A long shot that paid off. As Aunt Betty moved the story along towards World War II, I wondered if Father thought about the bottle and his own chances twenty years later when he was faced with the Order-in-Council from Ottawa.

I knew about the Evacuation, the internment camps and the Dispersal. The implications for me had disturbed me no end, but only now was I feeling the profound frustration of not being able to talk to my father. My hands curled into fists, whitening my knuckles. I will never know how he felt about what had happened.

Two months after December 7, 1941, Matsujiro Watada, labelled an *enemy alien*, received notification to leave his wife and son in Vancouver within two hours and travel a hundred and fifty miles inland to a construction site. Aunt Betty related that Father was given a shovel and told to build a highway. For weeks he laboured for a dollar a day, ten hours a day. At night, he had only the cold ground and a tent for comfort. He often woke up shivering, the outside of the canvas covered in morning dew.

In the meantime, my mother and brother were forcibly moved to Slocan. Aunt Betty and Uncle too. All communication was cut off. Perhaps then my father understood the misgivings and worry his grandfather, mother and siblings had had for him travelling to Canada, a distant land of white demons.

"After nine months, the Security Commission let him go and told him where we were." Aunt Betty coughed as she continued, "He joined us in Slocan in the dead of winter. The shacks had thin walls. The water froze …"

"Aunt Betty, you've really got to stop smoking," I complained.

"Never mind. I like smoking. Your father was a brave man. He was the one who said all of us must go east. Forget Vancouver. We could never live there again."

As I lay in bed that night, my aunt's words fanned the embers of stories I had heard over the years, stories that only now came to life. Gradually night moved into the single digits of the clock and my thoughts sank deeper into the darkness. I pondered the camps and what my parents had suffered. I couldn't imagine, but I did know Canada had treated them as enemy aliens. Took everything. Humiliated them into exile. Could Canada do the same to me?

Why not? I could have the wrong face just as they did. Could I lose my home? Could I be an *enemy alien*?

After a library visit the next day, I guessed that the Aleut who found the letter on some deserted beach must have been dumb-founded when faced with the same questions.

The Aleutian Islands were considered strategically valuable in the struggle for naval supremacy in the Pacific during World War II. Consequently on June 7, 1942, the Japanese attacked Dutch Harbor, near Unalaska, and occupied Attu and Kiska islands at the tip of the Aleutian chain.

The U.S. Department of the Interior reacted quickly. In an effort to "protect" the natives under their jurisdiction, the department ordered the military commanders in the area to evacuate 881 residents of the Aleutian and Pribilof islands. The Japanese had already taken 42 Aleuts prisoner at Chicagof village on Attu.

The Aleuts were given two hours to pack one suitcase and gather their families together for the move. But move to where? The government set up five internment camps in abandoned canneries in southeastern Alaska.

As the weather turned, wind and moisture cut through the cannery walls. The conditions were ideal for tuberculosis, pneumonia, influenza, measles and mumps. One out of every ten Aleuts died in custody. One death certificate listed the cause of death simply as "pain".

When my father reunited with the family in Slocan, as Aunt Betty had told me, they lived in a shack which was marginally better than the tent Father had pitched on unforgiving ground somewhere in the Fraser Canyon. After the war, the government demanded the Japanese move east of the Rockies. Dad and Mom worked as share-croppers in Alberta. A mean, hard time. They suffered grey drinking water, a chicken-shack house and miles of tundra-like landscape. Eventually, they settled in Toronto, never to see Vancouver again.

A week later, I rummaged through the mementoes a last time and found the album with the 1959 Japan trip photographs. Small,

square, black and white pieces of our lives together. In the major-
ity of the pictures, I stood in short sleeve shirt, shorts and a Tokyo
Giants baseball cap on my head. I always smiled with a *yancha-bōzu*
look on my face. My father in a light-coloured suit and my mother
in a print dress stood beside me, keeping me in line. A tight grip on
my shoulder, I remembered.

The last picture on the last page was of my mother's potted
plant. My father had written underneath it, "Home at last, flowers." The phrase glowed in my mind. The message of the bottle
suddenly became clear. Father's initial hope in this new land had
become realised. Even after abandonment, arrest, incarceration,
and exile, Canada had become home after forty years. My home.

> *The tall boy stood on the beach facing west over the green, slap-
> ping water. The wind was slight but enough for him to feel it
> against his face. In his fist, he held a tightly rolled piece of
> paper. He then rolled a second piece of paper into the first. He
> made sure the address faced outward. He pulled a soda bottle
> from his back pocket and twisted the message through the bottle
> neck. He sealed it with a cork and glue. Once again, he gazed
> across the smooth surface of water and imagined the depths. He
> felt the warm current, black and relentlessly moving towards ...
> towards home. Mother's arms. Sisters teasing him. The wisdom
> of elders. "Take me home," he whispered. He kissed the bottle,
> leaned back and heaved it through the crystal air and into the
> buoyant, thick water. He watched the bottle bob and weave
> through the whitecaps. Gulls spied it but thought better than to
> dive for it. Kuroshio-san is a good guide. I'm going home, he
> imagined.*

Over seventy years ago, a young man, homesick and blessed
with a vivid imagination, threw a bottle into the ocean. Contained
therein was a simple message, expressing his gratitude, his thrill at
the new, and his love for his family. And miracle of miracles, the
bottle found its way home via an Aleut, a hydrographer, and a
Navy captain in Washington just as my father found a home after

weathering the storms of history. Seventy years later, the message of the bottle itself has travelled farther still – across the wide gulf of death into the hands of that impulsive teenager's grateful second son.

Glossary

ah re/ah ra	masculine and feminine expressions of surprise: Heavens! Goodness!
ah, sō ne	expression: Oh, that's right.
ahō	foolish, stupid
Asahi baseball team	popular all Japanese Canadian baseball team, pre-WWII Vancouver team
Atsui ne?	expression: Isn't it hot?
baishakunin	a matchmaker
baka/bakayaro/ bakatare	a fool, an idiot; or, as an expression: You idiot!
bakemono	see Obakemono
bento	box lunch
bonsai	a potted dwarf tree
bonsan	a Buddhist priest
boro boro	ragged, tattered
bōshin	a boss
busaikuna	plain, homely
butsudan	a household Buddhist altar
-chan	form of address to children
chigo/ochigo	a child in a Buddhist parade; a catamite
chikushō	a curse: God damn it!
chikushō-dō	to degrade oneself to the level of devil beasts; a curse

Dannoura	site of decisive battle of Gempei War (April 25, 1185)
daruma	a round figurine representing a Buddha
Dharma	the teaching of the Buddha
dobuzake	bootlegged alcohol
fue	small wooden flute
furōba	a public bath
gaijin	a foreigner, an alien
gaman	perseverance
Ganbari-nasai	an expression: Stick with it!
Gempei War	Japanese civil war, 1180–1185
gohan	rice, a meal; or, as an expression: Dinner is ready!
gūru	Japanese pronunciation of English word: good
hakujin	Caucasian
hashi	chopsticks
hayaku	an expression: Hurry up!
hinotama	a fireball
hotokesama	ancestors
Idō	The Great Movement (the Evacuation)
inaka	rural
issei	immigrant generation of Japanese Canadians
jorō	a prostitute
jorō-ya	a house of prostitution
judō dōjō	a judo gym
kagami	mirror
karma	fate (colloquial)
kasu	dregs, grounds
kawaii	dear, loving, charming, cute

Kawaisō ne	an expression: Isn't that pitiful?
-ken	a prefecture
ketō	a white person (pejorative)
kichigai	madness, craziness, lunacy
kika-nisei	Canadian born Japanese Canadian educated in Japan
kimono	Japanese garment, a full set of formal clothes or casual attire
Kochi come ne	an expression which is a combination of English and Japanese: Come this way.
kōden	a monetary offering to a departed spirit, a condolence gift
koji	a tub for malted rice
Kojō-no Tsuki	popular song written by Bansai Doi and Rentaro Taki, 1900, the English being "Moon Over a Ruined Castle"
kokeshi	a limbless wooden doll
kuro-chan	a Negro baby (pejorative)
Kurogane	iron, term used in 19th-century Japan to refer to Admiral Perry's black ships (1853)
kurombo	a Negro (pejorative)
kusotare	son of a bitch (vulgarism)
ma	an expression of surprise: Oh!
ma ēyo	an expression: It's all right.
manju	a bun with a bean-jam filling
Maru	a title of an ocean-going ship (similar to H.M.S. or U.S.S.)
mi kudari han	a three-line note of annulment prevalent in prewar Japan
minyō	a folk song

miso shiru	soybean soup
mochi	pounded rice cake
mushi	an insect
Namu Amida Butsu	a Buddhist expression: I rely on the Buddha of Infinite Light and Life.
Naniyo	an expression: What?
-ne	an expression: You see. You know. Isn't it?
Nembutsu	an expression of gratitude to the Buddha (Namu Amida Butsu)
Nem-mind	Japanese pronunciation of English phrase: Never mind.
Nirvana	the perfect Buddhist state often confused with Heaven
nisei	second generation Japanese Canadians, the children of the issei generation
nombei	a slang expression: town drunk
obakemono/ bakemono	an apparition, a monster, a spook
obāsan	an older lady
Obon	Buddhist festival of light honouring ancestors
ocha	tea
odori	a dance
ofuro	hot bath, a bath house
Oi!	an expression: Hey!
ojuzu	a Buddhist rosary
okāsan/kāsan	mother
okayu	hot rice soup
Ōkiku natta ne?	an expression: You have grown tall, haven't you?
Okinasai	a command: Wake up!

onigiri	rice ball
onīsan/nīsan	eldest brother
Oshare ne	an expression: Such pretension!
otōsan/tōsan	father
otōto	younger brother
oyabun	a boss
Raku Raku	name of nightclub in prewar Vancouver: Pleasure Pleasure
Sa	an expression: So!
-san	a salutation: Mr.
saibashi	vulgarism, a cursing word. Term coined by the Japanese in B.C.
sake	rice wine
salarymen	contemporary Japanese term for businessmen
sangha	a Buddhist community or assembly
sensei	a teacher, a master
Shikataganai desho	an expression: It cannot be helped.
Shimatta	an expression: Damn it!
Shina-no Yoru	popular song during the 1930s: "China Nights"
Sō ka	an expression: Is that right?
Sō ne	That is right.
sonchō	a village chief
sutra	a Buddhist aphorism
taisho	a boss
tako	an octopus
tansu	a chest of drawers
Tatakeika hokoriga detekuru	prewar slang for a hidden scandal: Hit the back and dust will come out.

Hokoriga deta	past tense of expression: Dust came out
tatami	straw matting
tsunami	a tidal wave
waka	poetry
yancha-bōzu	mischievous boy
yare-yare	a sigh of relief: well, well.
yoshi	an expression: Okay.
yōshoku	Western cooking or food
yukata	an informal kimono for summer or bed
yūrei	a ghost

About the Author

Terry Watada is a writer who lives in Toronto between trips to Vancouver, San Francisco, New York or Honolulu where he takes great pleasure in his culture. His recent publications include *A Thousand Homes* (poetry) and *Bukkyo Tozen: A History of Jodo Shinshu Buddhism in Canada, 1905–1995*. He is also a playwright and a musician with three produced plays and eight record albums to his credit. He is particularly proud of his monthly column in the *Nikkei Voice*, the national journal for the Japanese Canadian community. He travels with his wife Tane and son Bunji.